Bellevue

Nebraska's Oldest Frontier Town

Wm. Bruce McCoy

BELLEVUE
NEBRASKA'S OLDEST FRONTIER TOWN

iUniverse books may be ordered through booksellers or by contacting:

iUniverse
1663 Liberty Drive
Bloomington, IN 47403
www.iuniverse.com
844-349-9409

ISBN: 978-1-6632-0230-7 (sc)
ISBN: 978-1-6632-0231-4 (hc)
ISBN: 978-1-6632-0229-1 (e)

Library of Congress Control Number: 2021902167

Printed in the United States of America.

iUniverse rev. date: 03/04/2021

This book is dedicated to my brother, Robert Wayne McCoy, who passed away on May 8, 2020. Bob was a gentle man, a hard-working man, a religious man, and a family man. He attended high school in Tecumseh, Nebraska, and graduated from the University of Nebraska in Lincoln with a degree in journalism. He had worked at the *Lincoln Journal Star* during his college years, and his first job after college was at the *Omaha World-Herald*. He married Antoinette Tucker from Albion, Nebraska, and soon after that they moved to St. Louis when he got a job at the *St. Louis Post Dispatch*. He spent the next fifty years working as a sportswriter and then sports editor for both the *Post Dispatch* and then for the national *Sporting News Magazine*. He left St. Louis during a strike and worked for about a year at the *Philadelphia Inquirer*, then returned to St. Louis to finish his career at the *Post Dispatch*. During the last several years of his work, Bob began showing signs of early-stage Alzheimer's, which he battled for many years before finally succumbing.

Bob and his wife, Toni, had four children, Tracy, Tim, Nicole, and Kitty. All four children still reside in the St. Louis area. Two of the three daughters are teachers, and the third daughter is a purchasing agent with a motion picture distributor.

Following Bob's retirement, they sold their house of joy in Webster Groves after living for forty years at the same location. They moved to a retirement center in St. Louis, and he later was moved to more of an acute care facility.

Bob was always an inspiration to me, not only when I was a child but also after we became adults and each had our own families. He was always very supportive of me, gave me extremely good advice, and was a real friend and confidant in time of need. He loved writing things, especially limericks. He always wanted his writings to make things either informational or enjoyable. Sometimes, they were both. I guess that now he will be forever immortalized by Gene Autry's famous song that could have instead been titled "Ghost Writers in the Sky." Write on forever, Bob!

Contents

Acknowledgments

I would like to acknowledge several people in my writing of this book, as well as several literary and research documents that greatly enabled me in writing this story of hope and survival in the settling of the American frontier.

I want to acknowledge several particular research vehicles and other organizations for the historical information in my book. Wikipedia was a major source of information for me. Google also provided me with considerable information. The Douglas County Historical Museum and the Sarpy County Historical Society provided information and pictures, as well as Linda Lewis's 1978 book entitled *Moses Merrill Would Be Impressed* and Ben Justman's 2011 book *Images of America: Bellevue*. Pictures were also obtained from *La Belle Vue* and *Bellevue: A Pictorial History*. Mervin Rees Photography authorized usage of the author's picture.

I started this book in the late 1980s when I was working as an administrator for the Bellevue School District in Bellevue, Nebraska. My special friend, Charmayne Hodnefield, picked up my short manuscript from the dust heap about three years ago and kept encouraging me to write some more. My daughter, Kathrin, also read it and encouraged me to finish it. But it took the pandemic, when I was isolated and had nothing to do, to make me finally take out the old manuscript and start adding more data and rewriting the original sections. It just kept growing and growing to get to the final product that I recently completed. When I finished, Char; my sister, Carol; and Kathrin were the first readers of my manuscript to correct my typos and wording and offer suggestions. Kathrin did an amazing amount of editing and made some solid improvement suggestions.

I would also like to thank all four of my daughters for their support throughout my educational career and life in general. They are Kristin, Karin, Kathrin, and Keenan. I would also like to thank their mother, Janet, for her immense part in raising them to be the people they are today.

Characters in *Bellevue*

Franklin Family
Matt
Amy
Sammy

**Matt's Family
in Kentucky**
Benjamin
Susan (mother)
Martha (sister)
Mary (sister)

Newspaper/School
Daniel Reed
D. E. Reed

Fontenelle Bank
Frank Cash
Lottie Cash

Wedding Party
Priscilla Byers—aka Prissy (maid of honor)
Mae Flowers (bridesmaid)
Bonnie Lassey (bridesmaid)
C. Worthy Leader (best man)
Harvey Forster (groomsman)
Claude Buster (groomsman)

Forster Family
Clint
Ruby
Becky
Harvey

Amy's Parents

Jasper Hughes
Caroline Hughes

Hardware Store
Brad Pincher
Penny Pincher

**Farmer/
Gardeners**
Ernest Gardner
Tillie Gardner

Post Office
Teresa Stamp

Wagonmaster
Billy Banks

Blacksmith
Henry Shorter

Preacher

Harper Devine

Ferry Company
Wilbur Ford

Trading Post
Barry Hyde (Peter
Sarpy's son-in-law)

Second Trail Guide
Willy Holmes

Shipping Company
Roger Lade (owner)
C. Worthy Leader
(captain)

Horse Seller
Stan Hardy

Drunk on July 4
Les Manners

The Wagon Train

$\mathcal{M}$att Franklin sat on his horse, Wanderer, atop a high promontory above the Missouri River and gazed out over the mighty river at the spectacular panorama that unfolded. It was just before noon on a spring day in 1857. Matt noted the trees and shrubs flowering along the water's edge on the far side of the river that added to the beauty of the scene. The breeze billowed Matt's shirt and rippled the tall grass as he studied the river. The river itself was already riding fairly high and moving swiftly due to the snow melts from the Tetons, Rockies, and other mountainous and elevated areas nearer to the source of this huge river.

Matt, a sinewy and very serious young man, shared the duty of being the lead scout for the wagon train with another man named Willy Holmes. For this week, Matt had the duty of being the lead scout, riding ahead of the wagon train to check the terrain and watch for alternative routes if any unexpected barriers appeared. This method was a procedure that the wagon train master, Billy Banks, had been incorporating into his scouting procedures for the last ten or so years on his wagon train ventures to the West. So far, it had proven to be highly effective and also allowed the lead scout to alert the rest of the group to potential dangers ahead.

Right now, Matt's attention was also focused on two figures moving along the riverbank. From this distance, they appeared to be Pawnee, but he couldn't be sure unless he saw them from a little closer distance. He hoped they were Pawnee because people of that tribe had proved to be friendlier than those of some other area tribes, and recently they had traded some goods with a small contingent of Pawnee men. He had heard that the Sac and the Otoe, or any other Indian tribe that might be in the area, were not as friendly to the settlers. He worried that an unfriendly group of Native Americans might place them in a vulnerable situation, subject to the danger of an attack.

He drew closer to where the two men were on the bank and saw that they, indeed, were Pawnee. He approached them with a peace sign and asked them if there was any game nearby so they might be able to get some meat for the wagon train and replenish their supply. The men gestured off to the west and indicated that a small herd of buffalo were in that area. Matt thanked them for the information, turned his horse, and headed back toward the wagon train, where he reported to Billy Banks that a buffalo herd was nearby.

The wagon train was now traveling in a general northward direction, following the meandering curves of the west bank of the Missouri River. The river had been dubbed the Mighty Mo already because of its huge volume of water and its reputation for mightiness during the spring flooding season. Flooding occurred almost yearly with the spring thaw, depending a lot on the volume of snow that had fallen that past winter in the Rockies, plus the amount of ice jammed up on the other rivers and tributaries that fed into the Platte River and other rivers that fed into the Missouri. The river always crept up its banks in the spring, and if the winter snow and resultant thaw were heavy enough, the river occasionally spilled over heavily into the nearby lowlands of the Nebraska Territory.

The group of wagons in this wagon train had left weeks earlier from Louisville, Kentucky; stopped at several locations in Kentucky, Indiana, and Illinois; and then stopped for a couple of days in St.

Louis, Missouri, before heading on west to Wentzville and making a couple of other short overnight stops on their way to Independence, Missouri. From there, they had headed northwest to St. Joseph, a rapidly growing trading stop off on the banks of the Missouri. They had ferried across the river at St. Joseph and headed north along the river, going past the Nebraska Territory settlements of Rulo, Brownville, and then Nebraska City, and just yesterday they had traveled past the little river community named Plattsmouth.

As Matt gazed at the beauty of the surrounding scenery, his thoughts drifted back to years earlier when he was growing up in the bluegrass country of Kentucky and his life there, where he had also been surrounded by beautiful scenery. His parents, Benjamin and Susan, had raised horses on a small scale, especially compared to some of the surrounding horse farms. Matt had two older sisters, Mary and Martha, whom he loved dearly but with whom he never really got too close, as they were only a year apart and best of friends. Matt was eight years younger, kind of like an afterthought by his parents. He had found various ways to entertain himself when he was younger and tried to help his dad with the horses as often as his dad would allow. He became an excellent rider and often went on long rides through their property and even to other properties. Matt was a friendly boy and rode around the area often, stopping to talk to neighbors about how their crops were doing and how their horses and other animals were doing. Most all the neighbors welcomed him and talked with him, but one owner who lived about three miles away, whom Matt had run into on one of his rides, asked who Matt was and told him never to ride onto his property again or he would have Matt arrested. This kind of frightened and worried Matt, so he avoided that farm as much as possible on his rides.

Matt thought about that man and his animosity for several days and then asked his father if he knew him and why he was so unfriendly. Benjamin said that, from the description Matt had given, the man was Jasper Hughes and that they had engaged in a rather bitter dispute several years earlier over the ownership of a few horses.

Benjamin had gone to a town about thirty miles away because he had heard that an owner there was selling or trading some young foals because his herd was growing too large. Benjamin had been told that the man would trade for grain or hay that he could use to take care of his remaining herd. So Benjamin had hitched up his wagon and stopped along the way to buy a large number of grain sacks, as well as some other utensils useful to horse owners. When he got to the other man's estate, they had agreed upon a fair trade, and Benjamin had returned home with four young foals and the excess grain he still had.

A couple of weeks later, Jasper Hughes discovered that he was missing several young foals from his herd, so he set out around the area to look for them. After a couple of days of searching, he happened to notice that Benjamin had some young foals with his horse herd. He confronted Benjamin, and they argued and even came to blows. Jasper refused to believe Benjamin's story, even though he was told where Benjamin had gotten the foals. He never did follow up on it and remained bitter toward Benjamin, feeling that he would never speak to him or try to patch things up for the rest of their lives. What none of them knew or even suspected was that, in actuality, a young rustler had stolen five of Jasper's young foals one night at just about the same time that Benjamin was arriving back home with the four foals he had bartered for.

After reflecting on those past events from many years ago involving Jasper Hughes, Matt then recalled the circumstances when he had met his wife, Amy. When he was almost seventeen years old, he had been out riding one day in the pasturelands in the vicinity of where they both lived. Amy's horse had thrown a shoe, and Matt had stopped to offer her some assistance, which she had gratefully accepted. He and Amy had grown up not too far from each other but had not really noticed or socialized with each other until then. Matt was a solidly built young man of above-average height and had dark hair. Amy was blonde and blue eyed and of medium height. They were almost instantly attracted to each other. Matt took out some materials from his saddlebags and wrapped the horse's hoof so that Amy could ride him back to their horse farm, where the farm farrier would take care of replacing the horseshoe. Just to be absolutely certain she was okay, and to spend more time with her, he rode beside her until they reached a hill overlooking Amy's home. As Matt looked toward her home, his mind told him that this was the property of Jasper Hughes, the man who had confronted Matt years before. He and Amy had already exchanged first names, so he asked her what her last name was. When she replied that it was Hughes, he was taken aback. He told her that his last name was Franklin and that their fathers hated each other. Amy also knew about the feud, and they discussed it and why it had occurred before concluding their conversation on that day. They had agreed that they should meet again to discuss the situation, and then they said goodbye and parted ways. They both agreed to ride out to the same location where they had first met three days later and talk again.

These meetings began to come about more and more often during the next year as they grew to know each other better and to, in fact, fall in love. Unfortunately, their meetings during this time continued to be clandestine because of the animosity their fathers had toward each other. Eventually, they asked their fathers to talk to each other and try to heal their differences, but try as they might, Matt and Amy could not get their fathers to contact each other and try to patch up their long-standing quarrel. Furthermore, neither father would give his blessing to Matt and Amy in regard to their continuing to see each other.

Finally, Matt and Amy decided that they were going to just go ahead and get married, hoping that this action would finally draw the families together. Instead, they both were immediately informed by their fathers that they were no longer a part of their families and must leave their homes. Even though their mothers both tried to intervene and pled with their husbands to relent, neither would do so. Matt and Amy packed up all their belongings and moved to a small room over the livery stable in Louisville, where Matt worked for the livery owner in return for room and board and a small wage. Amy also helped earn some additional money by taking in laundry and cleaning houses for people. They began saving as much money as they could from these wages, in case they needed a larger sum of money in the future.

After almost two years of this kind of life and with no change in their status with their fathers, Amy discovered that she was pregnant. As the time for the new baby drew near, they sent letters to both sets of parents but heard nothing back. When the baby was born, they sent news to the parents but still got no response from them. Upset and very disappointed that their parents had made no contact in regard to their new baby, Matt and Amy examined their alternatives. They could see no reason to continue their present existence when their families didn't want to see them and seemingly didn't care about them. They decided to leave Kentucky and travel west on a wagon train to Oregon, where they would start a new life for themselves by perhaps raising horses. They had saved up over a thousand dollars since they had been married, part of which they would use to buy a good wagon, horses, and supplies for the journey.

They planned to use the rest of their money to make a down payment on a farm when they reached Oregon and get started. Matt got a good deal from the livery owner on a wagon and three horses, and they waited for the next wagon train heading west to come through. When news arrived that a new group of settlers was in town, Matt went to them and talked to Billy Banks about joining up with his wagon train. First, they traded information about why they were both there at this time, preparing for a long trek west. Matt gave information regarding his skills and his background, and Billy indicated the kind of work ethic and demeanor that he expected of those who were going to be a part of the wagon train. Billy asked a few more questions and then agreed that they could join the group for the trip west.

Matt and Amy spent the rest of the day purchasing their supplies and loading the rest of the wagon, thanked their employer for his generosity and understanding, and sent letters to their parents informing them that they were leaving for Oregon. They then pulled their wagon into the long line of wagons and prepared to head out on the journey with Billy, which would eventually lead them to Oregon and their new life as horse ranchers or whatever other opportunities might arise for them.

Start of the Trek at Louisville

*M*att then began thinking about the starting site of the wagon train and of their various adventures, obstacles, and stops along the way on their journey. The train formed in Louisville, Kentucky, because it was rapidly becoming a very important city on the Ohio River and seemed like a good location for groups that wanted to head west to gather. There were about thirty wagons in the train, plus a chuck wagon and a couple of supply wagons. The big wagon train finalized its members in Louisville with members from the North Carolina and Kentucky areas, as well as assorted other travelers who had ended up in the location where the wagon train led by Billy Banks was going to become an official caravan. Louisville was a bustling and thriving community with all the necessary kinds of stores and shops to furnish the waggoneers with the supplies and materials that they needed. A couple of men in town helped finance these trips west, as they wanted to send supplies and goods out west in order to take advantage of the needs of the people already settled there and to promote their own commercial interests. Each time a wagon train returned from a trip west, these entrepreneurs would talk to the wagon masters and other people who had returned from westward journeys to find out what kinds of supplies were being requested for the next journey to the West.

Matt listened to as many people as he could, including the entrepreneurs, in order to help him decide just what the major purposes might be for their journey to the West. Personally, he wondered if he wanted to go in order to show his and Amy's parents that they could succeed on their own. Did they just expect to begin a new and different life? Did they just want to experience new scenery and grandeur? They also had to consider whether they really wanted to be that far away from family.

Louisville was founded in 1778 by George Rogers Clark. It was one of the oldest cities west of the Appalachian Mountains and was named after King Louis XVI of France. Due to the river travel obstruction caused by the nearby Falls of the Ohio, Louisville developed as a very necessary portage place. Lewis and Clark had organized their expedition west from the town of Clarksville, Indiana, which was just across the river from Louisville and near the Falls of the Ohio.

Ethnic tensions were often high in the Louisville area in the 1840s and 1850s. In fact, August 6, 1855, became known as Bloody Monday after Protestant mobs attacked German and Irish catholic neighborhoods on Election Day, resulting in twenty-two deaths. During the Civil War, Louisville became a major stronghold for the Union forces. Another highlight regarding Louisville later in the century was the first running of the Kentucky Derby on May 17, 1875, at the Louisville Jockey Club, which was later renamed Churchill Downs. The derby was originally shepherded by Meriwether Lewis Clark, the grandson of William Clark, one of the two organizers of the Lewis and Clark expedition. The Run for the Roses was conceived of and incorporated by a young man whose roots extended back to the early 1800s, when daring explorers, such as his grandfather, were out there in the West searching for not just the roses but trying to find an entire garden of exploration for American settlers and pioneers.

The journey west was expected to take from four to five months, depending on weather and other factors. Original journeys normally took from 140 to 160 days, but these times were cut down as better routes were found and many companies set up portage ferries at the rivers. Those ferries saved a lot of time, and saved a lot of lives as many had drowned in prior years trying to get their wagons across some of the big rivers.

In the same spirit of adventure and exploration, the wagon train departed from Louisville, heading predominantly in a light northwesterly direction toward the city of St. Louis on the Mississippi River. This was a total journey of approximately 260 miles.

Trail Stops from Louisville to St. Louis

*A*fter eight nights of camping overnight on the prairie at favorable locations near water sources and grazing, the wagon train arrived at Evansville, Indiana, and made it their overnight stop. They wanted to use this stop so they could replenish some supplies. Evansville sat situated on an oxbow of the Ohio River. The city then and today has often been referred to as the Crescent City or the River City. As a testament to the Ohio River's grandeur, early French explorers named it La Belle Riviere (the beautiful river). The area has also been inhabited by several indigenous cultures for centuries. This city was founded in 1812, when Hugh McGary Jr. purchased about 440 acres of land and called it McGary's Landing. In 1814, he renamed the village Evansville in honor of Colonel Robert Morgan Evans. The town incorporated in 1817. Evansville's biggest growth occurred in the years after the Civil War. The city was a regular stop for steamboats along the Ohio River and a home port for many companies engaged in trade along the river.

After purchasing needed supplies, the wagon train got a late morning start the next day and again camped out in favorable locations on the prairie for five nights. The sixth day out of Evansville, they arrived at Mt. Vernon, Illinois, which was founded in 1817 by Zadoth Casey. It was named after the plantation of George Washington in Virginia. When originally founded, there were no roads into the town. In 1820–21, Ben Hood and Carter Wilkey built a bridge over Casey Creek, to the southeast of town. Soon, other roads were built, and Mt. Vernon became an important stop on the road west. In 1836, Joshua Grant came to Mt. Vernon from Kentucky with several of his sons and daughters. Three of the daughters and one son, Angus, from this wealthy family decided to remain in Mt. Vernon when their father and the other family members headed on toward Texas. Angus became an extremely important cog in the development of the town.

The next morning, the wagon train again hit the road and two days later arrived in the diminutive village of Fairfield, Illinois, where they again stayed the night and stocked up on more provisions. Fairfield was a town of about two hundred people in the early 1850s. It was known as a town of very friendly people, so the wagon train got along very well with them that evening as many people gathered around a big campfire, where they were roasting a cow and a pig for a big feast for all the wagon train members, as well as all the townspeople. Later on, in the early 1900s, the city gained notoriety when gang leaders Carl, Earl, and Bernie Shelton made Fairfield a household name in the region because of their bootlegging activities. They were also convicted of a mail carrier robbery in 1925. Friendly handouts had changed to not-so-friendly robberies and illegal distribution of spirits.

The wagon train left Fairfield and traveled seven more days before reaching the town of Belleville, Illinois. Camping out for six nights on the prairie made the entire wagon train eager to see some friendly people again. The name *Belleville* means "beautiful city." George Blair named it in 1814. It was incorporated as a village in 1819 and became a city in 1850. It became a coal mining area in 1874 when a huge deposit of coal was discovered. By 1879, 90 percent of the city's population was either German born or of German descent. Today, it is the eighth-most populated city in Illinois outside of the Chicago metropolitan area.

The next morning, they headed out early and, making good time, reached East St. Louis, still on the Illinois side of the Mississippi River. As it was rather late in the day, they decided to camp overnight on the Illinois side of the river and then be ferried across to St. Louis the next morning. St. Louis proved to be a very interesting and thriving town, and the wagon train decided to stay there for an extra night to explore some of its many places of interest. St. Louis was founded in 1764 by fur traders Pierre Laclede and Auguste Chateau. They named the town St. Louis, after King Louis IX of France. France ceded the area to Spain the next year after being defeated in the Seven Years War. Spain ceded the land back to France in 1800, and in 1803, the United States acquired the territory as part of the Louisiana Purchase, which French explorers Louis Jolliet and Jacques Marquette had explored in 1673. In 1678, La Salle claimed the region for France.

The St. Louis area was the center of the Native American-Mississippian culture, which built numerous temples and residential mounds on both sides of the Mississippi River. Steamboats first arrived in 1817, greatly improving trade connections down the Mississippi, all the way to New Orleans. In 1821, Missouri was admitted to the Union as a state, and in 1822, St. Louis was incorporated as a city. This very important early settlement was enhanced by its strategic position on the Mississippi River. It was also just fifteen miles south of where the Missouri River empties into the Mississippi. The combined length of the Missouri and Mississippi make them the fourth-longest river system in the entire world.

Other sidelights for the St. Louis area included the building of the Eads Bridge in 1874, connecting St. Louis to East St. Louis in Illinois. East St. Louis is now named Alton. The Eads Bridge goes from the area near Laclede's Landing and the present-day

Gateway Arch area over to the Illinois side of the river. The Eads Bridge was the symbolic emblem for the city until 1965, when the Gateway Arch was completed. The arch is 630 feet tall and is the world's tallest arch. Another major attraction for St. Louis is the Missouri Botanical Gardens, founded in 1859. Famous people who are linked to St. Louis include Charles Lindbergh and August Busch. Lindbergh was living in St. Louis in 1927, when he had just gotten financial backing from some businessmen to attempt the first nonstop transatlantic flight from New York City to Paris. Several men had tried it previously and had all failed. A hotel owner named Raymond Orteig had offered a $25,000 prize to whoever accomplished the feat first. Lindbergh left New York City on May 20, 1927, and thirty-three and a half hours later, he landed in Paris. One hundred thousand people were there to greet him when his plane, named *The Spirit of St. Louis*, landed. Lindbergh grew up on a farm in Minnesota, attended the University of Wisconsin where he studied aviation, and made his first solo flight at Lincoln, Nebraska, in 1923. In 1924, he joined the army and made airmail flights as an army reservist from St. Louis to Chicago. He had many more daring aviation exploits, earning the nickname Lucky Lindy. Many years after Lindbergh's death, President Calvin Coolidge awarded Lindbergh the Distinguished Flying Medal.

August Busch Jr. was an American brewing magnate who built the Anheuser-Busch companies into the largest brewing company in the world around 1957. Busch also obtained ownership of the St. Louis Cardinals baseball team during his tenure with that company. Another famous person from St. Louis is Bob McCoy, who spent just over fifty years there as a sportswriter and as a sports editor for the *St. Louis Post Dispatch,* and at a different time, he was the sports editor for *Sporting News* magazine. McCoy won several writing awards and also worked in the St. Louis Cardinals baseball organization for many years.

The wagon train members camped near Laclede's Landing, and they dispersed to the various shops, trading posts, saloons, and even a brothel. Matt and Amy took Sammy to a nearby café to eat, and they strolled the streets of St. Louis, following along the west banks of the Mississippi River. It seemed to be a very interesting and thriving settlement. After returning to camp that night, many stories were related about all their many daytime adventures, except for those who wanted to keep their more clandestine adventures for the day to themselves.

Trail Stops from St. Louis to St. Joseph

*T*he next day, the wagon train headed west again. After two long days of travel on a very flat and easy-to-travel surface area, they neared the small village of Wentzville, Missouri. Wentzville had only been laid out in 1855 and had been named after the chief engineer of the Northern Missouri Railroad, Erasmus Livingston Wentz. Wentzville went on to grow and prosper and developed into a very successful community and city, especially after the interstate system was built through Missouri and I-70 was routed right past Wentzville.

After spending the night camped near Wentzville, the wagon train continued west, again making good time except for two days when it rained quite heavily and the train was forced to abandon its journey for those days and hunker down out of the elements. This stay was also accentuated by the death of one of the women, who got soaked to the skin. This hypothermia, coupled with some previous ailments, caused her to be unable to breathe properly, and she died. The entire wagon train participated in a service for her, and they buried her there on the prairie, with a small headstone citing her name and life span. Even with this delay, they arrived at the town of Columbia after seven days and camped nearby, again with the goal of refilling some depleted supplies.

Columbia was founded in 1821, with a settlement of pioneers from Kentucky and Virginia in the early 1800s. They settled in a region known as Booneslick, where Daniel Boone had lived and done his hunting and trapping. The county where he had lived was founded and named Boone County in 1820, shortly after his death. Boone's Lick Road was also named after him during this time period.

Before 1815, settlement in the region was pretty much confined to small wood forts because of the threat of Native American attacks both before and after the War of 1812. The city was incorporated in 1821. Despite prolonged settlement rates and logistical delays, Columbia College was founded in 1839, and it later became the University of Missouri. With its emphasis on learning and education, the town of Columbia along the way earned the nickname the Athens of Missouri. Log cabins made up the majority of houses in the village of Smithton, which later became a part of Columbia. Columbia's first mayor, in 1820, was Richard Gentry, a trustee of the Smithton Company.

After traveling nine more days across Missouri, the wagon train arrived at Independence. The town had originally been inhabited by Missouri and Osage Indians, followed by a Spanish tenure and then a brief French tenure. It became part of the United States with the Louisiana Purchase of 1803. Lewis and Clark stopped there in 1804 and recorded in their journals the stop and the accompanying details. Independence was named after the Declaration of Independence and was founded in March of 1827. As more settlers arrived during westward expansion, Independence became known as the Queen City of the Trails because it was a point of departure for California, Oregon, and the Santa Fe area. Independence was a logical place for a wagon train to stop because of its strategic location and its many goods and services. Independence was the furthermost point west on the Missouri River where steamboats or other cargo vessels could travel due to the convergence of the Kansas River with the Missouri River approximately five or six miles west of town. Independence quickly became a hub for the fur trade. Interestingly, in 1831, members of the Latter-Day Saints began moving there under the leadership of Joseph Smith. Smith actually declared a spot west of the Courthouse Square to be the site of his prophesied temple of the New Jerusalem, in expectation of the Second Coming of the Christ. But he and his followers were driven from the area in 1833 and moved on west to eventually settle in Utah.

From Independence, Billy Bank's wagon train headed northwest since they were going to Oregon. The next big settlement they arrived at seven days later was St. Joseph, named after the biblical Saint Joseph (which seemed quite coincidental). Billy had been with Joseph Robidoux, a local fur trader returning from the west in 1842. Robidoux officially founded St. Joseph in 1843. It was a bustling frontier town and became the jumping-off point for what was called the Wild West and for the Oregon Trail. The town was the westernmost point in the United States that was accessible by rail until after the Civil War. Three other interesting sidelights about St. Joseph are that it was the starting point of the Pony Express, the famous outlaw Jesse James was killed there, and the eight main east-west streets in town were named after Joseph Robidoux's children: Faraon, Jules, Francois, Felix, Edmond, Charles, Sylvanie, and Messanie. It appears as if Robidoux didn't spend all his time out fur trading and trapping.

Trail Stops from St. Joseph to the Current Day

*A*fter ferrying across the river at St. Joseph, the wagon train traveled up the Nebraska Territory side of the river and in five days arrived at a little settlement called Rulo, which was being laid out the year the wagon train arrived there, 1857. Rulo was named after its original owner, Charlie Rouleau. The town is of interest primarily because, in 1933, the foundation for a toll bridge across the Missouri was laid. The owner of that new bridge would be John Mullen from Falls City, together with a group of investors called the Kansas City Bridge Company. Construction of the actual bridge began in 1938 and was finished in 1939, with half the funds coming from the Works Progress Administration (WPA). Rulo also had a dark side at one time, as it had an infamous group of Christian identity survivalists who settled just north of the town along the river. They became infamous robbers of the nearby Kansas, Nebraska, and Missouri areas and used the money from the sale of their stolen goods to buy weapons and survivalist equipment. Their leader, Michael Ryan, was arrested and convicted of the murders of two cult members, a twenty-six-year-old man and a five-year-old boy, and he spent the rest of his life in a Nebraska prison, dying there in 2015.

The next settlement stop for the wagon train was called Brownville. Established in 1854 and incorporated in 1856, it was at that time the largest city in the Nebraska Territory. It became a very important port on the Missouri. The rise of the railroad after the Civil War became Brownville's downfall, as it diverted a great deal of shipping away from the steamboats on the river. In 1939, the Brownville Bridge was built across the Missouri River, and today it is listed on the National Register of Historic Places. Thomas Tipton was a long-time US senator from Brownville, and the touring boat called *The Belle of Brownville* was built in 1967. Today it is in Omaha, Nebraska, and is called *The River City Star.*

The next stop was in the community of Nebraska City. It had taken longer than expected because they had run into an old acquaintance of one of the wagon train members from New York, a young journalist by the name of Julius Sterling Morton, who had headed west in part to start a newspaper in the territory. He had established the *Nebraska City News* in 1854 and now had been appointed as the territorial secretary for the Nebraska Territory, a post he would hold for four more years, until 1861. They had run into Morton at the trading post and exchanged pleasantries for a while, and Morton insisted that they stop by his new estate on the north edge of the community so that they could get some fresh horses for the remainder of the trip, as well as other staples that he had an excess of at that moment. Two years earlier, Morton had built a mansion on the grounds that he had purchased shortly after his arrival in the area. He called his estate Arbor Lodge because of all the trees he had planted on the property. Arbor Lodge was a fifty-two-room mansion with an adjacent livery and beautifully manicured gardens. Eventually, hundreds of tree varieties were planted on the property. In 1857, however, the plantings and the estate itself were in their early years. No one was aware of it at the time, but Morton's arboreal ambitions led to his establishing Arbor Day in 1872, which became a legal holiday in the country on April 22, 1885, the same day as Morton's birthday. His knowledge of trees and vegetation, as well as his prominence in the territory in the late nineteenth century, led to Morton's being named secretary of agriculture by President Grover Cleveland, a post he held from 1893 to 1897. Morton's son Joy later became the founder and namesake of Morton Salt. Another son, Paul Morton, served as secretary of the navy under Theodore Roosevelt after his earlier service as vice president of the Santa Fe Railroad.

Nebraska City also produced other notable figures in American history. John Henry Kagl became second-in-command in John Brown's historic raid on Harper's Ferry in 1859. He also created a station for the Underground Railroad at Mayhew's Cabin in Nebraska City, which was known as John Brown's Cave. Other notables from Nebraska City include Joe Ricketts, the founder and long-time owner of Ameritrade, and his son, Pete Ricketts, who is presently the governor of the state of Nebraska.

Matt, his family, and all the other members of the wagon train were thoroughly enchanted by the Arbor Lodge estate and the many things planted on its grounds, and they talked about it excitedly after they had enjoyed Morton's hospitality for the better part of two days and nights. Matt had a couple of very good conversations with J.

Sterling Morton during those days and gained some perspective on life in the Nebraska Territory. On their final day there, he noticed a seemingly flamboyant conversation involving Morton, Clint Forster, and a couple of other settlers, with Clint's son, Harvey, kind of listening to the conversation from the fringe. Matt, himself, could only hear a few of the tidbits and comments that were being exchanged.

Arbor Lodge and its grounds, main building, and museum are still standing today, open for visitors, and it is a very historical and interesting place to stop and browse.

A week after leaving Rulo, the wagon train had wound its way to Plattsmouth. Plattsmouth first appeared as a place called The Barracks in 1854, a trading post established by Sam Martin, who owned the Platteville Ferry, which was headquartered across the river in Iowa. In 1855, the settlement renamed the town Plattsmouth due to its location near the mouth of the Platte River, where it empties into the Missouri. The Plattsmouth Main Street is on the National Register of Historic Places.

The wagon train hit the trail again at the crack of dawn and headed northward again, toward the Platte River. As they started rolling the wagons northward, Matt rode his horse on out ahead, scrutinizing the terrain and taking note of anything unusual that should be reported back. He rode ahead to find the best route for the wagons and about every hour rode back within eyesight of the wagon train to signal them as to what direction to continue. He then repeated the pattern, riding his horse out in front of the wagon train group again. It was on his latest scouting circuit that he had come to the promontory that provided him with such a pleasurable and inspiring view of the mighty river and of the vegetation along the edges of the river. It was also where he spotted the two Pawnee men who were seining along the riverbank.

The Franklin and Forster Families

*M*att's wife, Amy, and their two-year-old son, Sammy, were back with the wagon train. Amy did an excellent job of driving their wagon and keeping the horses moving. However, while Matt was out scouting, it was difficult for Amy to drive the wagon all day and still watch Sammy and keep him happy and entertained. For that reason, Amy had been joined on the wagon this week by Becky Forster, the nineteen-year-old daughter of Clint and Ruby Forster, other wagon train members. Becky was pretty and of medium height and often had her dark hair in braids. Amy felt that she could talk to Becky about anything and kind of viewed her as the sister that she had always wanted to have. Becky's younger brother, Harvey, was sixteen years old and a strapping redhead, who was also rather quiet. The Forster family had joined the wagon train group to go west after a racial problem back in North Carolina. Clint and Ruby had decided to pack up all their worldly belongings and head west to make a new life for themselves in Oregon. Clint hoped to take advantage of his many skills in Oregon and set up a blacksmith business upon their arrival there. Clint was a hard-working, honest man with craggy features. He could fix anything that was broken or malfunctioning and had often helped other members of the wagon train with broken wheels or axles, torn canvases, and broken yokes on their wagons. Clint was a real wainwright. (A wain is a wagon, and a wainwright is a person who works on and fixes anything that is wrong with a wagon.) His son, Harvey, worked right alongside his father on most of these jobs and ventures and had become very skilled himself with his hands. They had also heard about the vast amounts of timber in Oregon and figured that their combined skills could also be put to good use in the burgeoning lumber industry if the blacksmithing plan did not work out.

Back in Clarksburg, Virginia, in the mid 1830s, Clint had been a jack of all trades, making repairs to wagons, shoeing horses, building sheds, and doing other assorted jobs. Ruby was the schoolteacher at a small log cabin school that took care of a usual group of eight to twelve students each year. One October, Ruby could not get the old stove to work, so she asked someone to have a reliable person come fix it. That person had Clint go to the school and make the necessary repairs. Sparks began flying with Clint as he became quite attracted to the young schoolmarm, and after that he continually found reasons to visit the school and to help fix little things that were eventually going to need repair (or so he told himself). Ruby was not fooled by Clint's interest in the school, but she found that she, herself, was becoming increasingly attracted to this hard-working and helpful man. They continued courting for about a year and then got married. Their savings were used to buy a small acreage just outside of town. Their daughter, Becky, was born in 1838 and their son, Harvey, in 1841. Becky became a very industrious and likable person with a great deal of determination, and Harvey grew to be a strong young man, rather shy and quiet, but nevertheless very likable.

In and around Clarksburg were various farms and plantations. Some had slaves, and some did not. Clint and Ruby were antislavery but kept it to themselves as much as they could, not wanting to stir up any unnecessary arguments or problems. Then one morning in 1855, just before dawn, Clint heard someone knocking on their door. He went to answer it and found a man standing there who said that he had heard that the people in this house were against slavery and that he wanted to know if that was true. Clint was somewhat taken aback, not knowing exactly what the purpose of the man's visit was, so he was very careful in his response. He said that he did not own any slaves and did not intend to do so. The man looked at him very closely and speculatively and then asked Clint if, in case any escaped slaves ever stopped by his house, he would allow them to hide there for the day until the next evening when it got dark. Knowing that his answer could have negative repercussions either way, he simply said that he would allow people to rest at his farm if they were on a journey. The man again looked at him closely and then said that he had three runaway slaves with him who were hiding in the trees behind the house and asked if they could they stay in his barn until nightfall. Clint, having already discussed this scenario with his wife, said that they would allow the runaways to rest in the barn for the day. He met the man and the three runaways, two men and a woman, in the barnyard, took them into the barn, and showed them some stalls where they could rest. He brought some blankets for them to use and then went back into the house to inform Ruby. She quickly went to the kitchen to get some food for the entourage now in the barn and took it out to them. Shortly after that, she dressed and went into town so she could be at the schoolhouse when students arrived. Clint then got Becky and Harvey up, gave them breakfast, and informed them of what was happening with the visitors. He said that helping them was the right thing to do but that they themselves were to stay away from the barn and never let on to anyone that they were now a small part of the Underground Railroad.

The Underground Railroad allowed thirty thousand slaves to escape to freedom between 1840 and 1860. "Conductors" would go onto plantations, posing as someone looking for runaways or as a slave sent from another plantation, and talk with the slaves during the day.

In this manner, conductors could determine who would be trustworthy to keep a secret and also strong enough to attempt the journey toward freedom. From this point, the conductor would line up their departure for one of the next nights. As part of their plan, dedicated conductors and slaves seeking freedom would leave under the cover of darkness and travel anywhere from ten to twenty miles during the night before reaching a safe haven sometime before dawn. These safe havens became known as stations or depots and were spread out in numerous locations between the slave states and the free northern states or Canada. The depots could be a barn, a tunnel along a riverbank, a cave, or under the floorboards of some portion of a house or church. The Ohio River was viewed as the River Jordan as a boundary between slave states and free states. Slave escapes to the North really escalated after 1849, when Harriet Tubman, from the eastern shore of Maryland, escaped to Philadelphia. Clint and Ruby had heard of Tubman and her many trips back into Maryland to rescue more slaves. That area of eastern shore Maryland where Tubman worked her magic was not too far from where Clint and Ruby lived, only about a hundred miles away. They had wondered aloud to each other if Tubman might ever make a foray down into their vicinity and discussed what they might do in such an instance. They were highly impressed and influenced by her actions and commitment to her cause, and they followed her triumphs and remembered her courage and bravery. Tubman returned again and again to the Maryland area to rescue slaves during the ensuing dozen years, interrupted only by the breakout of the Civil War, during which she enlisted and participated as an armed guide. During this time, she became the first woman to lead an armed expedition, as she guided the raid at Combahee Ferry, which liberated seven hundred slaves. During the years between 1849 and the end of the Civil War, Tubman became known as Moses by most people as she delivered her people out of bondage. She was also called Minty, a derivative of her original name, which she later changed to Harriet. Historians record her unfailing successes as a conductor on the Underground Railroad—she is never known to have lost a passenger.

As a result of this first act of assistance, Clint and Ruby's farm became a regular stop on the Underground Railroad for the next year or so. By then, much civil unrest and fury had arisen over escapees, and regular bounties were placed on runaways, along with bounties on those people who helped them to escape. With this situation creating a great deal of anxiety and wanting to remove their children from any possible danger in being recognized as traitors, they decided late in 1856 to leave their farm behind and head west. Their plan was to go to Louisville, Kentucky, to meet up with a wagon train that was heading west so they could start a new life. Louisville was fairly easy to get to, as all they needed to do was follow the Ohio River until reaching the town of Louisville. They knew a few other people in town who were sympathetic to the Underground Railroad. They found a man who had no family to purchase their farm from them so that he could take up the cause of helping the runaways. They packed up their belongings into wagons right after Christmas and departed for Louisville early in January. During this particular era in Virginia, the state conducted a vote in 1861 to secede from the union. The northwest section of the state voted heavily to not secede; therefore, the secession vote for the overall state did not pass. Following that, a large contingent of northwest Virginia voted to withdraw from the state of Virginia, and the state was officially split, with the new section becoming known as West Virginia. In 1863, the state of West Virginia was officially admitted to the nation, bringing Clarksburg, Clint and Ruby's old town, into the union.

Once on the trail as part of the wagon train, Becky and her mother shared in doing all the cooking for the family and also washed and mended all their clothing. During the performance of these daily duties, Becky had developed a close friendship with Amy Franklin. As they worked on things together, Becky had also become very fond of Matt and of their youngster, Sammy, who, in return, loved Becky dearly because she always played with him and told him stories. Therefore, he was delighted that Becky had been riding on the wagon with them for the present week while Matt was out front scouting. Sammy was constantly chattering and trying to get whoever was not driving the horses to play games with him. The only respite for the adults was when he got tired and fell asleep for a while. Then they could talk to each other about matters that they wished to discuss.

Becky's feelings toward Matt were more than casual, but she kept them to herself. His pleasant manner, his helpfulness, his politeness toward her, and his rugged good looks all made her attracted to him in a way she'd never before been attracted to a man. But she had no one to share her thoughts with about this because of her love and respect for Amy. She was content to just be friends with the couple and to simply admire Matt in her own secret thoughts. On these days, with Matt out ahead of the wagon train scouting, it was easy for all kinds of conversation to come up between Amy and Becky, especially while Sammy slept or was otherwise occupied with playing. At present, Amy had just finished reading to Sammy until he had drifted off to sleep, and she now was back up in front in the wagon, talking to Becky. Amy began telling Becky about Matt's gentleness and caring during their lovemaking the night before, not realizing the discomfort it was causing Becky. Becky tried to listen unemotionally and at the same time show her understanding of Amy's feelings, but it tugged dramatically at her heart to do so. She sat quietly and listened while Amy recounted the events of the past night and told why she thought Matt had been so tender and sensitive. Finally, Becky couldn't stand to listen any longer, so she tried directing her thoughts toward something else and would occasionally say something to Amy to indicate that she was still listening, although she wasn't. Their wagon kept moving forward at a steady pace, with Amy going on and on about Matt's attributes and other things of a personal nature, with Becky entering into some of the conversation but turning her thoughts elsewhere when the discussion turned to things about Matt that troubled her and made her uncomfortable.

Up ahead on the promontory, Matt's attention was diverted from the swirling river and the nature surrounding it when there was a sudden little burst of cool air. He looked up to see that the sky was beginning to cloud over. Big thunderheads were already beginning to appear on the western horizon, and he could see that farther up the river to the north and also over to the northwest it was raining already. He needed to judge the severity and the duration of this upcoming storm and plan for the wagon train to make camp if necessary. He rode quickly up to the next rise, and about a quarter of a mile ahead of his location he spotted a large grove of trees where the wagons would receive some amount of protection if the storm grew more intense.

It was now beginning to sprinkle, and as he glanced at the sky farther north, he could see the clouds becoming vastly darker and more threatening. Lightning was streaking across the sky, and thunderclaps boomed and sounded menacing in the distance. Matt concluded that they were in for a big spring storm. He turned his horse to ride quickly back to the wagon train to get them moving more quickly forward. He wanted the wagon train to reach the protection of the grove of trees he had just located. He reached the wagon train within minutes. After Matt explained the approaching threat of the storm to Banks, the veteran wagon master quickly started the wagons moving forward at a faster pace so they could reach the protected area that Matt had located. In a very short period of time, everyone was moving quickly forward.

The Onset of the Storm

The heavy spring thunderstorm was a downpour and had already been driving down relentlessly for over thirty minutes by the time all the wagons got situated within the protection of the grove of trees. All the settlers sat huddled under the canvas of their various wagons. There had not been time to pitch any tents because it was already raining extremely heavily by the time the first wagons reached the protection of the trees. The trees were helping some in cutting the force of the wind, but the volume and strength of the rain was such that no one could venture outside, even under the trees, without becoming soaked to the skin. No one could remember a more intense rainstorm since the wagons had left the Louisville, Kentucky, area. The force of the wind had also recently made the temperature fall markedly, and many of the settlers had blankets wrapped around them in an attempt to stay warm.

The wagon master, Billy Banks, was a grizzled veteran of several trips west to the Oregon territory. He had proven to be an excellent leader due to his determination, courage, and intuitive sense of doing the right thing at the right time. When Matt had ridden back to the wagons with the recommendation to seek cover, Billy had already analyzed the skies and determined they were about to experience a severe storm. When Matt told him about the grove of trees, Billy quickly sprang into action and got his wagons moving forward at a brisker pace. When they reached the trees, Billy had ridden around feverishly, getting wagons situated in the most strategic places and then helping get horses tethered and in some cases took their harnesses off. Matt had worked right along with him, and by the time they had gotten all the wagons into formation, both men were soaked and very tired. Billy told Matt to go to his own wagon to check on his family and change clothes. Billy headed for his own wagon to do the same. After getting into dry clothing, he pulled out a bottle of whiskey and poured himself a stiff drink. The liquid quickly warmed him and began to take some of the chill from his bones.

Matt had tied his horse at his wagon and gone into the wagon to find that Amy and Sam were okay and that Becky was still with them, keeping them company. She really hadn't had much choice in the matter, however, without getting soaked by trying to get to her own wagon. Besides, she thought it best to keep Amy and Sam company rather than go to where her parents and brother were under the stormy conditions. Matt asked her if she would mind staying for a little while longer so that he could go to confer with the wagon master, and she agreed to stay until he got back. Matt hung a blanket across the inside of the wagon, changed into some dry clothes while screening himself behind the blanket, and then excused himself to go see the wagon master, promising to be back as soon as possible.

When Matt arrived at their leader's wagon, he accepted a half glass of whiskey from Billy, and then the two began to discuss the effect of the storm on their plans that day and in the days upcoming. They were nearing the confluence of the Platte River and the Missouri River, where they would cross the Platte and go to Bellevue, an important settlement south and east of Omaha. They would travel to Bellevue, meet up with new wagons there, and then continue on their westward trek to Oregon. Normally, Billy's wagon train would have taken a northwesterly route from Independence to Fort Kearny, but this time they had traveled north to meet this other small group so that the settlers from the Omaha and Bellevue area could travel with them, thus making the entire group larger and better able to protect themselves.

The Platte River was a major river in the Nebraska Territory. Measured from the source of its farthest tributary, the North Platte River, the Platte is over one thousand miles long, and the Platte itself is a tributary of the Missouri River. The Platte and its tributaries drain a large portion of the Central Plains, originating from the eastern Rockies in Colorado and Wyoming. The river valley played a major part in the routes of wagon train trails, namely the Oregon, California, Mormon, and Bozeman trails. It was named the Platte from translations of Otoe tribe and French explorer words that basically mean "flat river." In Nebraska, the Platte forms near the town of North Platte, Nebraska, near the confluence of the North Platte and South Platte rivers. Those two rivers rise from the snowmelt of the eastern Rockies, east of the Continental Divide, and they flow on down to meet the Platte at the town of North Platte.

Varying cultures of indigenous people have lived intermittently along the Platte River for thousands of years. The Indian tribes typically visited different areas during different seasons, following the bison herds for their hunting, in order to provide a major source of their food. Before 1870, herds of several hundred thousand bison (buffalo) periodically migrated across the Platte River in order to follow their seasonal grazing. Today, the numbers of bison on the Great Plains has been greatly diminished, mostly trampled by the greed of settler hunters and fur traders.

Anyway, the Platte was right then rising to much greater heights than normal as the waters from the Rocky Mountain melt and the western Nebraska Territory melt all rushed down their respective tributaries to the main channel of the Platte. The swollen river continued to rise higher and to make a mighty roar as it continued heading in an eastward direction, past forts and towns, gathering strength and destructiveness as it went. This imminent flood could not only be a major deterrent to the wagon train's efforts to get across the Platte River, but it could prove dangerous to both the settlers and their draft animals.

Billy's Life and Wagon Train Formation

As their discussion continued, the rain also continued. Gradually, their discussion moved away from the plans for the continued trip, and they got around to discussing their personal pasts as well as their plans for the future.

Billy had started his wagon-train-leading experience over fifteen years earlier. After his third glass of whiskey, Billy confided that he had been engaged to be married back in Pennsylvania, but two nights before the wedding he had discovered his fiancée in a compromising situation with another man. He had become enraged and had severely beaten the other man. When he finally regained his composure, he realized that the other man was lying on the floor bleeding and unconscious, and Billy had panicked. Thinking the man might be dead, Billy had left his sobbing and hysterical ex-fiancée standing in the room and ran out of the building. The next morning he happened upon a wagon train that was departing for points west, so he signed up with them as a scout and sentry, deciding it would be a good idea to get away from the area in case he had, in fact, killed the other man. Billy loved that trip west and the return trip back east in 1842. He traveled part of the way back with Joseph Robidoux, the fur trader who founded the city of St. Joseph, Missouri, the next year. After spending the winter in Wyoming, they crossed Nebraska to the Missouri River, using the Oregon Trail that had been established by Robert Stuart in 1812. Billy became very proficient and knowledgeable on that trip.

When they arrived back east, Billy returned cautiously to the Pennsylvania area where he had assaulted the other man and discovered that he had not killed him. With this knowledge, he considered staying. But then a businessman who had heard about his valiant and innovative exploits on his trip to the West with the last wagon train talked to him about becoming a wagon master for a wagon train that was going to carry goods and supplies west to the frontier settlers. Billy quickly accepted the job offer. It had proven to be a very successful trip for Billy and a profitable one for the businessman, who not only hired Billy again for other trips but also gave Billy's name to other people looking for a solid and knowledgeable wagon master for trips to the West. Billy's future had then been determined, and he had been very successful in fulfilling this kind of work. The present trip with the settlers heading for Oregon was Billy's fourteenth trip as a wagon master since the time he had done the first one those many years ago.

Next it was Matt's turn to confide in Billy why he and Amy had joined the wagon train. He reflected on their reasons. Billy listened attentively and considered offering no comments, but then he decided to ask Matt if he had really thought about whether he wanted to not only go this far away from his parents and family but also to leave Amy's family so far away from them. He could see that this gave Matt a little time to pause and reflect, but Matt did not respond to the question. As they finished their conversation and Matt headed back to his own wagon, Billy still wondered if this was really a journey that Matt and Amy should be making.

The Omen of the Thunderstorm

*A*fter about seven hours of hard rain, the storm abated. The group had no way of knowing, but almost eight inches of rain had fallen not only where they were but also upriver on the Missouri and to the northwest, along the route of the Platte River. Combining with the spring snow thaws, especially from the Tetons and Rockies, tons of water were roaring down the Platte River toward the Missouri. The Missouri itself was now bank high or higher as it headed past the Ponca and Omaha Indian campgrounds, past DeSoto Bend, past the abandoned Fort Atkinson, and on toward the settlement of the Omaha area. These waters were rushing in torrents both on the Missouri and on the Platte, heading for the confluence where those two rivers meet. Both the Platte and the Missouri were running over their banks and roaring through the surrounding lowlands. Their roaring sounded like rumbling thunder, and the swollen waters were dumping tons of silt and debris on what had previously been the banks of these two rivers.

The Deluge

*A*s quickly as it had started, the spring storm came to an end. The sun began breaking through the clouds, and as the settlers climbed out of their wagons, white, glinting shafts of sunlight sparkled down through the wet leaves of the trees. Almost at once, the air became humid, and vapor began to rise off the grass and trees.

Everyone hitched up their horses to their wagons and pulled on ahead to a clearing at the top of a rise where their things would dry out faster. They all formed a big circle for the night. Down below them, they could see the swollen Platte River roaring by and heading onto the Missouri. Some of the settlers then began to tend to their horses, while others began gathering sticks and wood in order to get cooking and heating fires started. People from every wagon began to hang out clothing and blankets to dry, as these had all become drenched by the storm.

The Forster wagon ended up in the circle right next to Matt and Amy's. While Amy was hanging up blankets and clothing to dry, Becky accompanied three other women downhill to the river to get some water. The hill was slick, and they realized they would not be able to go back up that way carrying full buckets of water. Once they arrived at the bottom of the bank, they noted that the level of the river was extremely high, actually even surging over the top of the bank. They quickly gathered their water and started back to the wagons by a slightly different route about fifty yards south, where there was a gradual ascent back up to the plateau. Becky looked back and saw Sammy, who had come down the hill following her. She set down her buckets and ran back to get him, carrying him back to where the buckets were sitting. She grabbed the buckets and told him to hurry along next to her until they got to the slope of the hill where they began their ascent to the plateau. Behind her she could hear a loud roaring noise that was getting even louder.

Up by the wagons, Amy finished hanging clothes out to dry when she looked around and noticed that Sammy was nowhere to be seen. Harvey Forster was feeding and rubbing down the horses at his wagon, so Amy asked Harvey if he had seen Sammy go by. Harvey said, "Gosh, I'm sorry, but now that you mention it, I think I saw him go down the hill toward the river after Becky went down there to get water." Amy became a little hysterical and began yelling, "Sammy! Sammy!" as she went running down the slope toward the river, slipping and sliding on the muddy bank. As she reached the bottom of the hill and continued calling Sammy's name, she became vaguely aware of a loud roaring noise, like thunder, off to her left toward the northwest. As she reached the edge of the river, she saw no one. Glancing around, she saw four women, including Becky, just reaching the top of the plateau about fifty yards downstream. She started running in that direction, yelling, "Becky, do you have Sammy?" Becky heard her and turned to confirm that Sammy was with her, when to her horror she saw a huge wall of water bearing down on Amy from behind. Becky screamed at the top of her lungs, "Look out! Run up the hill!" As Becky yelled, Amy turned slightly toward the onrushing water, and then the wall hit her. Tumbling and screaming, she was carried away downstream by the relentless torrent of water.

As the raging water passed about twenty feet below where Becky was standing, Becky screamed for help as loudly as she could and grabbed Sammy into her arms, covering his eyes and ears as much as she could. In a flash, many settlers crowded around, and Becky was sobbing about what she had just witnessed. Another lady took Sammy from her arms and carried him away from the commotion, as Sammy whimpered and cried because of all the confusion going on.

Matt came running up, and upon hearing what had occurred, he screamed in anguish and began running downstream alongside the river with the dim hope that somehow Amy had been dumped ashore by the raging water. After running almost a mile and seeing nothing but the swirling water and its assortment of debris, Matt sank to his knees and began sobbing uncontrollably. The love of his life was gone, and their dream for a future together in Oregon was shattered.

Billy got his horse and rode downstream, where he found Matt on his knees. He looked at him sympathetically for a short time, and then he went over and helped Matt to his feet. He cradled him in his arms and then helped him get on the horse. Billy then got up on the horse behind Matt and put his arms around him to grab the reins and also to hold Matt in the saddle. Matt's grief began slowly abating as they rode back to the camp. When they got back, Clint Forster was there to help Matt dismount from the horse, and both he and Billy held Matt's arms until they reached the wagons. Becky ran out to them and wrapped her arms around Matt, crying uncontrollably. "Matt, I'm so sorry. My dear friend Amy is gone!" was all she could say. Together, they stood and held each other in their time of grief, while others in the wagon train gathered around and tried to console them. Eventually, the men helped Matt to his own wagon, while the ladies took Becky to the Forster wagon and helped her to calm down and get settled for the night. Young Sammy was being cared for by another lady and had already been put to bed. As Matt and Becky got settled, everyone else went to their own wagons in hushed moods to settle down for the night.

The clouds cleared and the stars and moon were shining brightly, but they shone down on a somber and eerie setting, where scarcely a whisper could be heard in the stillness of the night. As Matt sat in his wagon in a mood of desolation, he reflected on the stillness outside and also began to think about the futures of him and of his son.

A Time for Grieving

$\mathscr{T}$he next day was a Friday, and it dawned bright and sunny with no hint of the raging storm they'd seen the afternoon before. The wagon train would stay camped in the same place for the remainder of that day, partly out of compassion and respect for Matt so he could find some time to properly grieve, partly because the next day started the weekend, and partly to figure out the best way to ford the Platte River and get into Bellevue.

The same procedure of taking a day off for a funeral had occurred back between Wentzville and Columbia a month or so earlier, when a woman died and they stayed the day to have a service for her and to bury her. This episode was very different, in that there was no body to bury and no grave to dig. But they would still allow Matt to grieve.

Billy had sent a scout, Willy Holmes, out late the previous afternoon to check the terrain and look for a place where he could get across the river and ride on up to Bellevue. Once he got there, he would secure the ferrying services of the Peter Sarpy Ferry Company, which had begun operating between Bellevue and St. Mary's, Iowa, eleven years earlier, in 1846. The next morning, they would have a memorial service for Amy at 11:00, conducted by Billy. If Willy was back by the time of the service, Billy would also give them the plan for when they would continue their journey to cross the Platte River and get to Bellevue, where they would meet up with other settlers who would be joining the wagon train going west.

Just after the crack of dawn, Matt arose, dressed, saddled up his horse, and took off down the slope to the banks of the Missouri River, where he followed it south for several miles searching for Amy or any remnants of clothing or anything that he felt might help relieve his pain and give him some closure. He found nothing of help, and finally, after almost three hours, he gave up the search and headed back to the camp to prepare for Amy's memorial service. He would gather up Sammy, and they would go to the service together to say farewell to his wife and Sammy's mother.

At 11:00, all the wagon train people gathered around a big clearing for the memorial service. Billy walked out to the front and gave a short talk about Amy, her devotion and dedication to her family, and her grit as she managed their team of horses day after day. A couple of women then offered up some Bible readings and some prayers. During the Bible readings, Willy returned to the camp. After the prayers, Billy reported that Willy had arranged for the ferry to be at the confluence of the Platte and the Missouri Rivers at 8:00 a.m. on Sunday morning and that the wagons should be in line near the south edge of the Platte at that time. The group then made their way past Matt and Sammy to express their condolences. It was very hard on Matt, especially seeing the confusion on Sammy's face as he accepted people's condolences while at the same time looking around and wondering where his mommy was.

The Forster family had come over by Matt and Sammy to give them some additional support. Becky did her best to keep Sammy engaged in what was happening and at the same time show her support for Matt. After all the other wagon train members had filed through, Matt and Sammy and the Forster family went back to where their wagons were parked next to each other and began preparing lunch. The rest of the day was spent with the entire wagon train getting things ready for their trip across the Platte and then on to Bellevue. They were anxious to get to Bellevue, which had been touted to them by many people as a very progressive frontier community.

Becky offered to keep Sammy overnight and to entertain him so that Matt could be alone with his grief, if that was what he would prefer. Matt accepted her offer and spent the evening thinking about all that had happened since he had met Amy while out riding horses five years previously. He also thought about his family and pondered what he should do at this point. He knew that he had to send them a letter explaining the situation. He also reminded himself that he needed to inform Amy's parents of what had happened and to get those letters mailed while they were in Bellevue. So he sat down that evening and began composing them, while he also began thinking about the journey west and whether he really wanted to continue without Amy. He continued writing and thinking until after eleven o'clock that night, at which time he went to sleep.

The next morning, which was Saturday, he continued composing the letters and considering his next step. Without Amy, the reasons for going had changed. There could no longer be a new life together. He would now be going to Oregon with only Sammy and taking them farther away from family.

He spent most of the day alone, allowing Sammy to remain with the Forster family. He thought that would actually be better for Sammy, and it would also give Matt some time to think about his future. Around suppertime, he retrieved Sammy and took him back to their wagon. As he prepared to settle down and sleep, he was beginning to become certain that he no longer wanted to go onward to Oregon. As he prepared to go to sleep, he summoned the courage to face a big day ahead of them the next day.

The Platte River Crossing

*E*veryone on the wagon train was accustomed to being up at dawn or just after in order to get the day started. The next morning, which was Sunday, was no exception. It was a bright morning with lots of sunshine and little wind. The chuck wagon cook started a campfire at the crack of dawn and had coffee and some breakfast items prepared for the wagon train members soon after that. He kept his open-air café open until about a quarter until seven and then started cleaning it up and preparing his own wagon for the day's journey. At 7:00 a.m., a big bell was rung to tell the people to start getting their wagons into a line heading for the south bank of the Platte. Willy had been appointed as the lead scout that day so that Matt would be free to drive his own wagon. Becky had agreed to ride with Matt to help keep Sammy entertained.

The Forster wagon pulled into the line near the front, with the Franklin wagon right behind them. They were in place near the riverbank at seven thirty. True to the man's word, the Sarpy Ferry Company had its ferry round the bend into the confluence a few minutes earlier than scheduled. It pulled over to the south side of the Platte and began the process of ferrying all the wagons to the other side. Fortunately, the day was bright and calm and the river itself was also calm, so the ferrying process went off with few problems. Getting everything ferried across the river took about five hours. The wagon train then started for Bellevue, expecting to be there by late afternoon.

As they rode toward Bellevue, Matt and Becky conversed from time to time whenever Sammy was not pestering them too much. Eventually, Sammy drifted off to sleep, and Becky placed him on the floorboard and put a blanket over him. Matt and Becky could then share a little more conversation. Before then, they had been a bit afraid to discuss some things with Sammy listening. The major topic they had avoided discussing was Amy.

Matt revealed that, on the previous day, he had given everything a lot of thought and had pretty much made up his mind to stay in Bellevue and not proceed to Oregon with the wagon train. He mentioned the dreams and plans he and Amy had discussed and how this tragedy had destroyed those plans. He mentioned that his family back in Kentucky would not be quite so far away if he stayed in Bellevue. Becky mainly just listened as Matt revealed his new plans, but her mind was racing with thoughts of dismay and disappointment. Her main disappointment was that she had grown to love Sammy almost as much as if he were her own, and she also had a great deal of fondness and respect for Matt. She tried to give Matt positive encouragement to do what he felt he needed to do, but at the same time she was torn about what she herself was going to do. One thing she did know was that she should discuss all this with her parents and her brother that night.

Around five thirty that evening, the wagons rode over a small hill, and there, nestled down below them, was the town of Bellevue. As the wagons circled to make their camp that evening, all the people who were part of the wagon train knew that they would proceed into Bellevue the next day, see what was there, purchase some supplies, enjoy a meal, and see what else the town had to offer.

(Courtesy Nebraska State

Bellevue

*S*ettlement of what later was named Bellevue began when a fur-trading post was built in 1822 by Joshua Pilcher, who at that time was president of the Missouri Fur Company based in St. Louis. Pilcher sold his trading post in 1828 to Lucien Fontenelle, and it was renamed Fontenelle's Post. Fontenelle was a representative of the American Fur Company, and this post served as a central trading post with local Omaha, Pawnee, Missouri, and Otoe tribes. Different historians credit either Pilcher or an early Spanish trapper named Manuel Lisa with calling the settlement Belle Vue because of the beauty of the view from the bluffs overlooking the Missouri River. Lucien Fontenelle's son, Logan, was an extremely highly regarded Omaha Indian leader who spent most of his life in Bellevue but was killed by the Sioux in 1855 near Petersburg, Nebraska, while on a hunting trip. Logan Fontenelle had been active in the development of the town. Today, one of Bellevue's middle schools is named after Logan Fontenelle, as are the Fontenelle Hills housing community and Fontenelle Forest. The modern Fontenelle Forest is a fourteen-hundred-acre woodlands in the northeast part of Bellevue, with roughly twenty miles of hiking trails and abundant wildlife and plant life.

After the fur trade began declining a bit, Fontenelle sold the post in 1832 to the Missouri River Indian Agency (also called the Bellevue Agency). When Baptist missionaries Moses and Eliza Merrill arrived in 1833, the US Indian agent let them stay temporarily at the post.

In 1835, the Merrills moved with the Otoe about eight miles to the west, where they established what was known as the Otoe or Moses Merrill Mission. The Merrills started a school for the Indians, which was the beginning of a formal educational system in the Bellevue area. In 1839, Moses Merrill left the area to obtain treatment for consumption and died the next year, in 1840. Eliza Merrill tried for a period of time to keep the school going, but she could not manage it successfully by herself, so she took their child and left the wilderness. In the same year of 1835, log cabin homes were built on the floodplains down near the Missouri River. Due to cholera in the area, as well as the repeated danger of flooding, one of those cabins was moved in 1850 in its entirety up the hill about a mile west and then north to what is today 1805 Hancock Street. It is still located there and is said to be the oldest existing residence in the state of Nebraska. It was added to the National Register of Historic Places in 1970.

In 1842, John C. Fremont and Kit Carson completed their exploration of the Platte River Valley and then arrived in Bellevue. Fremont sold all his wagons and horses to local people once he got there.

The Presbyterians, under Samuel Allis and the Reverend John Dunbar, had advanced to the forefront of education in Bellevue. They had taken over the schooling at the old mission but could not be effective in that location, so the Board of the Mission then built a new mission house overlooking the river, completed in 1848. This huge building was used for many things, including school classes and church services. Various Indian children from the Pawnee, Omaha, and Otoe tribes attended the school, but the number of white settlers' children began to increase. But with Nebraska becoming an official territory in 1854, the government signed a contract with the Native Americans under which the tribes forfeited their lands near Bellevue and were awarded other lands in other locations. In 1856, the building of the historic Presbyterian church began at what is now 2002 Franklin Street, and the church was completed in 1858. It still remains there today and is the oldest church in the state of Nebraska. No longer used for church services, it is now owned by the City of Bellevue and has a historical marker in front of the church.

Peter Sarpy was an important person in the history and development of Bellevue. Born in St. Louis in 1805, he was of Creole descent, with his ancestors' hailing from Louisiana. At age nineteen, Sarpy traveled to Council Bluffs, Iowa, to work for the American Fur Trading Company, right across the Missouri River from present-day Omaha and roughly ten miles north of Bellevue. Sarpy developed and owned several fur-trading companies along the Missouri, with his main trading posts at Bellevue and at Decatur, Nebraska. During those years, he also laid out the plats for the towns of Bellevue and Decatur and developed a thriving ferry business, with companies at several places along the Missouri, including Bellevue and Decatur. During his later years, he resided in the Bellevue and Plattsmouth areas, and he died in Plattsmouth in 1865. He was influential in developing Bellevue and the surrounding area, and eventually the area that contains Bellevue and much of present-day Papillion was renamed Sarpy County by the State of Nebraska.

Sarpy was one of the most important developers of river ferries. In 1836, the first migrant wagon train headed to Oregon left from the town of Independence, Missouri. Early wagon trains had to build rafts at the larger rivers in order to get their wagons across. These crossings were often difficult and sometimes dangerous. Many lives were lost from drowning at such portages. In the Great Migration of 1843, wagon trains began carrying lumber for rafts on a special supply wagon.

The river ferries were instrumental in cutting down on the time needed to travel west and also in reducing the number of deaths caused by dangerous river crossings on rafts. The Mormons were well-known ferry builders and managed several crossing sites—one was at Fort Casper, Wyoming, and another was on the Green River near Fort Bridger. Ferries were also established on the Missouri, Kansas, Little Blue, Elkhorn, Loup, Platte, South Platte, North Platte, Laramie, Bear, Snake, John Day, Deoschutes, and Columbia Rivers. With the advent of ferries, the travel time was cut back from 140 to 160 days to just 120 to 130 days. Settlers were charged from three to eight dollars to use a ferry. Peter Sarpy's two most prosperous ferries were at Bellevue and Decatur, and he greatly increased his wealth because of them. You could say they were his ferry godmothers!

Bellevue was incorporated in 1855 and is the oldest continuous town in the state of Nebraska. The Nebraska Legislature credits Bellevue with being the second-oldest settlement in Nebraska, second to Fort Atkinson, which was located about twenty-five miles north of Bellevue. Bellevue was once a major seat of government in Nebraska and was once strongly considered to become the state capital. Today, it has a population of over fifty thousand people.

The Decisions

The night that they arrived to camp just outside Bellevue, everyone had supper at the chuck wagon and then began settling down for the night. In the Forster wagon, Becky worked up her nerve and then told her parents that she needed to talk to them. She told them all that Matt had said on their trip that day and that it seemed almost certain that Matt and Sammy would now remain in Bellevue and not continue to Oregon. She expressed her dismay at this circumstance, citing her extremely close relationship with Sammy and his need to have a mother figure around. She also stated that she felt close to Matt and did not want to desert him in his time of need. But she also said that she did not want to lose her family by staying behind while they went on to Oregon.

Both Becky's mother and father tried to help her consider information regarding both sides of the situation. Becky's mother, however, was very intuitive and had suspected for quite some time that Becky had a more-than-passing interest in Matt, and she knew that Becky absolutely loved little Sammy. She and her husband discussed it a while longer with Becky and then decided that they would discuss it all more tomorrow and try to get things settled then, as the wagon train was staying at the Bellevue site for the entire next day. As Becky's mother lay there later that night, trying to sleep, she suddenly got an idea that made her smile, and she vowed that she would work out the details of her brainstorm the next day.

The next morning, after breakfast and morning chores, Ruby Forster headed down the hill toward town. She began asking store owners about needs for teachers at any schools in the area and who she might talk to about them. She then went to the blacksmith shop to see if it might need an experienced and talented handyman. As it turned out, the blacksmith, Henry Shorter, stated that he had just lost a good worker who had moved away. She mentioned Clint and all the skills that he possessed, and the blacksmith seemed quite interested. Then, Ruby asked the blacksmith how to get to the mission house where school was held. He also told her that she might check first at the nearby office of the local newspaper, the *Bellevue Palladium*, because its editor, Daniel Reed, was also a teacher as well as an administrator at the mission school.

Daniel Reed was instrumental in the early development of the town. In addition to being the newspaper editor and a teacher and an administrator at the school, he had also served as the town postmaster since the opening of the new post office in 1856. Henry gave Ruby directions to the newspaper office and also to the mission school, and she began walking toward the newspaper office.

When Ruby arrived at the Bellevue Palladium, Daniel Reed was there doing some final editing on the weekly newspaper before it went to press. Ruby explained that she had been a teacher back in Virginia before they headed west and also explained the circumstances that they were in at the moment, due to their friend's death. Daniel said that the school had been having a small increase in enrollment during the last year or so, after he and his wife took over the management of the mission building in 1855. There had been a big drop in enrollment two years earlier when the Omaha tribe all moved to the Walthill, Nebraska, area. He said that they planned to continue the school year at least through the end of June, due to so many parents working during the day, and that he and his wife were now strongly considering adding even more time to the school year. They were also thinking of adding another new teacher, but he didn't know if they would be able to pay her very much.

The Omaha and Otoe Mission at Bellevue.
From the Past.

They discussed the possible amount that was offered, the time of day during which Ruby would need to be at the school, and other terms of the agreement. Ruby said that she would need to talk it over with her family and asked Daniel when she would be able to start work, if her husband and family agreed to her doing so. They then agreed that Ruby would show up at the mission school in two days at 8:00 a.m. if she wanted the job. Ruby thanked Daniel for his time and then walked over to look at the mission school itself in order to be better prepared for all contingencies. She arrived and found that it was a relatively large, two-story, white building directly overlooking the Missouri River. After checking out the mission and standing on its grounds, gazing at the Missouri River flowing along down the hill from the mission, she got a feeling of contentment and thought, *This would be a beautiful place to live and work.*

She then stopped back at the blacksmith shop and told Henry, the blacksmith, where she had been and all the information she had gleaned. She told him that she would speak with her husband that evening about working at the smithy and that she felt very strongly that things would work out and that Clint could work there. This news pleased Henry, and seeing that Ruby was quite tired, he asked her if she would like to take one of his horses home for the night and bring it back the next morning with a final answer. She thanked him and accepted his offer. He saddled the horse for her, and she headed back to the wagon train camp.

That evening, the family was all gathered in their wagon after supper to discuss the day's happenings. Ruby had not really told any of them of her plans for the day prior to that evening. The only comment anyone made to her when she returned that afternoon was Clint saying, "Where did you steal the horse?" She had responded that she borrowed it in town from the local blacksmith and was to return it the next morning. She also said that the blacksmith had offered Clint a job and that he should think about the prospect of that until after supper, at which time the family needed to have a discussion regarding their future plans.

Immediately after finishing their suppers at the chuck wagon, Ruby and Clint told Becky and Harvey that they needed to immediately return to the wagon to discuss some critical issues. Becky was playing with Sammy at the time and started to object, but her mother told her it was extremely important that they go have this discussion, that she thought it would end up being a good thing for all of them. Intrigued, Becky said goodbye to Sammy and Matt and followed her parents to their wagon.

As soon as they got to the wagon and sat down, Ruby relayed the information she had learned that day while she had been in Bellevue. Clint listened very carefully to the entire story and made no immediate comments. Initially, Becky started out listening to her mother rather cautiously, expecting something that she was not going to like, but as it all dawned on her, she began to have a feeling of incredulity and even of extreme hope. Harvey just listened. He did not appear to have any emotions one way or the other. As Ruby got to the end of her announcements, she said that she was now going to make a recommendation for the family and that they should all vote on it together. She said that she felt strongly that the family should stay in Bellevue. Clint would have a job at the blacksmith and would be able to move on into additional responsibilities. She herself would be able to teach at the mission school and continue in the vocation that she had loved doing for many previous years. Becky would be able to find various kinds of work and also be available to help Matt with Sammy. Harvey was a hard-working and skilled young man who would have no trouble finding meaningful work. Clint, who had been told of the blacksmith's offer a few hours earlier, said that he thought Ruby's recommendation was a very good and well-thought-out idea. Becky agreed, gushing with her effusive praise of the idea. Harvey shrugged his shoulders and said, "Whatever." They counted his indifference as a yes, and it was unanimous for them to stay in Bellevue. Before they told Matt or any others, Clint said he wanted to go tell Billy because it would mean having one less wagon in the train for protection. Fortunately, the train would be adding several wagons in Bellevue that were joining the westward venture. Clint said, "Stay here and do not tell anyone until I get back." He then went to find Billy.

Clint found Billy out in the middle of the wagon area and asked if he could speak privately with him. They wandered off to the side among the trees, where no one else was around. Clint informed Billy of their decision to stay in Bellevue, adding that work was available there for both Ruby and him. Billy listened carefully to what he had to say and then said that he understood their decision and had actually been kind of expecting it. He told Clint that Matt had informed him earlier in the day of his decision to stay in Bellevue, and Billy knew how close Becky was to both Sammy and Matt. Billy also knew that the Forster family were good friends with Matt, so he had wondered if they might also decide to stay. Billy thanked Clint for all his prodigious skill on the trail with helping fix broken wheels and axles and torn canvases on some of the wagons. He told Clint that whenever he was close by to Bellevue on one of his future trips, he would stop and look him up to see how things were going. They shook hands and parted ways.

Clint then stopped at Matt's wagon on the way back to his own and informed Matt of their decision. Matt seemed quite pleased with it and appreciative of their decision, stating that it would be much easier on him to have some people around that he knew and that he was glad they had made that decision. Clint informed Matt that Ruby had gone into town that day and that it appeared that both she and Clint would have jobs available in town. They talked a bit more and then, equally committed to a new life in Bellevue, they agreed to go into the town the next day to look for places to live and for employment opportunities for Matt.

Clint then returned to his wagon and informed his family that Billy had been receptive and understanding. Becky started to get up and leave, so Clint also told them that he had stopped to inform Matt of their decision and that Matt should have a chance to digest that and to perhaps also discuss it with Sammy. So Becky sat back down, and Clint told the group that they would all go into town together the next day to look for places to live. This was a major factor in their decision—whether there was any housing available and, if so, whether it was not only affordable but also usable. Also, they wouldn't know anyone as yet, but that had been true back in Louisville, too, and things had worked out fine.

Arriving and Getting Settled in Bellevue— Tuesday

The next morning, after having breakfast and saying goodbye to all the wagon train members they had gotten to know, Matt and Clint got their horses hitched up to their wagons, and the two wagons proceeded down the hill into town, leading the blacksmith's horse. They went straight to the blacksmith shop, where Clint introduced himself to Henry, and they exchanged pleasantries. Clint outlined all the experience that he had in all matters related to being a blacksmith. Clint also introduced Matt to Henry and said that Matt would also be looking for some kind of work, and he asked Henry if he knew of anything that might be available. Henry gave them a couple of ideas for work, and then they asked him if he knew where there might be some available housing. Henry also gave them some ideas on that. Henry and Clint reached an agreement that Clint would start the next day, if he could make suitable living arrangements that day. Otherwise, his start of employment could wait until a day or two later.

While Clint and Matt were talking to Henry, the other four took a little walk around the town and stopped at the newspaper office. Ruby talked with Daniel Reed, and he said that he had talked with other adults working at the school; they all said that Ruby would be welcome to start there as soon as she had settled into the community. He told Ruby that the children usually arrived at the school around nine o'clock in the morning and stayed until about three o'clock. The children had been off of school the day before and that day due to a scheduled break. Ruby then mentioned Matt to Daniel and asked him if he knew of any available jobs. Daniel said that he would give it some thought, talk to some of the town leaders, and get some ideas from them. Becky also told Daniel that she would be interested in doing some part-time work, if there was anything like that available, and that her brother would be willing to be hired out to someone as a handyman when he wasn't going to school.

From the smithy (the blacksmith shop), Matt walked across to the post office to mail the two letters he had prepared for his parents and for Amy's parents. The clerk, Teresa Stamp, informed him of the proper postage amount, and he left the letters with her to be delivered to Kentucky. He had been both understanding and diplomatic in his two letters and felt that he had not only done the right thing but also had done it diplomatically and with a sense of understanding for the feelings and emotions of Amy's parents.

The group then took their two wagons a short distance east and then headed north on a different street about a half mile to an area where there was a small log cabin and also a small house not too far from the cabin. The cabin had been moved there from the lowlands down by the river in 1850. The other house had been built by earlier settlers, who had since moved on to another locale. Both places looked rather austere, but they seemed to be in good repair and were not all that far from each other, so the group discussed whether they should check into purchasing them and who would want which one. Both Matt and Clint's family had ample savings to purchase a home there, as that was what they had been planning to do in Oregon. The wooden house was a little bigger than the log cabin, so it was decided that the Forster family should try to procure that house, and Matt would opt to purchase the log cabin.

They then went in search of the owners of those buildings to try to work out a deal. The log cabin home was owned by the local bank, as the previous owner had sold it to the bank when he left town, having been unable to sell it to anyone else. The other house was owned by the local hardware store owner, who had built himself a bigger house in town after living in that house for several years. He had then allowed two different families to stay in the home for a fee, but he was really more interested in selling it.

After thoroughly examining the exterior of the house, Clint went to the hardware store to talk to the owner, Brad Pincher, and his wife Penelope. He introduced himself and explained his situation, indicated that he was interested in living in the little house that Brad and Penelope owned, and asked for the sale price. Clint also indicated that he intended to not only work at the smithy but also do some repair work around town and said that he would be a regular customer for the hardware store. Of course, that last part interested Brad more than the occupation of the house. He gave Clint a purchase price for the house, but Penelope, eyeing Clint as a mark, interrupted and said that figure was too low. Townspeople had already given Penelope the nickname of Penny due to her constant dickering about prices. They thought that she really was a penny pincher. Brad and Clint negotiated for a little while, and then Brad said that his original price would be honored if Clint wanted to accept it. Clint had the money needed to purchase, so he agreed to that amount. They shook hands on the agreement with the understanding that Clint would first be able to look at the house and its interior to see how much work needed to be done on it. Brad left the store under his wife's care and followed Clint and his family to the house so that they could inspect the interior.

They went inside, and while the women looked at the kitchen and bedrooms, Clint inspected the walls, ceiling, and floors, particularly looking for evidence of leakage from the roof. He saw very little that appeared to be a major problem and the women seemed satisfied with what they had found, so they agreed upon the sale at a cost of two hundred and fifty dollars. Brad gave them permission to immediately take possession and begin moving their stuff in from the wagon. Of course, Brad knew that the Forster family would undoubtedly be coming back to his store for furnishings for their new residence. He gave them the key, said they could work out the details and the payment the next day, and returned to his hardware store. Clint and his son began carrying the heavier items from the wagon into the house, while Ruby and Becky brought in the smaller items and the things that were less wieldy.

Matt took Sammy and went to the town bank, which had opened the year before as the Fontenelle Bank at a different location, had failed due to a financial panic, and had reopened early in 1857 at a different location on Main Street. He asked for the bank manager, Franklin Cash, who came out from a back office, and Matt told him that he was interested in purchasing the log cabin or living there for a fee, and the banker's eyes lit up with anticipation. He was at least quite pleased to have a customer there who was interested in that property, as it was a rather small space and one that no one had been interested in for two years. Matt said that he had just arrived in Bellevue and planned to live in the town. Franklin quoted Matt a sale price, and Matt replied that he would have to see the interior of the unit before he could consider making an agreement. The banker's comment that he had not been able to find an occupant for the past two years was concerning to Matt, as he didn't want to purchase a home that would need extensive repairs and renovation. The banker agreed to show him the log cabin and its interior, so he told the cashier what time he would be back to the bank and rode with Matt to the log cabin.

They went inside, and Matt looked at everything thoroughly. He was pleasantly surprised to find that there was only some minor damage to part of the ceiling and to a couple of walls. There was ample room in the place for Sammy and him and a nice space outside where Sammy could run and play. Matt said that he realized it needed some work, and then he offered the banker a hundred dollars for the property, half of what the banker had asked. The banker countered with one hundred fifty, but they agreed on one hundred dollars with the stipulation that Matt would use the bank to keep his funds for a minimum of one year. Matt was planning to bank there anyway, so he accepted that offer. He realized that this might tie up his money if he needed it during the next year for unexpected expenses, but he wanted to get off to a good start in the town. They returned to the bank, where the banker filled out the proper bill of sale while Matt completed the paperwork to open an account at the bank. Matt gave the banker three hundred dollars—one hundred for the cabin and two hundred to open his account. The banker gave him a copy of the bill of sale and the key to the house, and Matt and Sammy returned to their new home, where Matt began taking things into the house that he felt they would need that evening.

Over at the Forster house, the family had gotten most everything into their new home, probably before Matt even got back to his house after dealing with the banker. After using buckets of water to wipe down everything in the kitchen and dining areas, Ruby began to rifle through things, looking for something to fix for their supper. Harvey had gone out with an ax and a saw to cut some fallen tree branches into wood sections that would fit into the stove in the house. They stoked a fire in the stove, and Ruby began cooking the food they had brought in from the wagon. When it was ready, they all sat down around an old table that had been left there and had their supper. After they finished eating, Ruby fixed a basketful of food and told Becky to take it over to Matt's log cabin in case they hadn't had a chance to eat as yet and to see if Matt would like for Becky to watch Sammy for a while. Becky grabbed the basket and hurried as fast as she could over to Matt's cabin.

Matt was still bringing things inside, and they had not yet had a chance to eat. Matt had already brought in a small folding table and some folding chairs from the wagon, so they set those up, and after Matt washed up, he and Sammy tore into the food. While they ate, Becky got a bucket and began to wash down the counters and walls of Matt's cabin. After their supper, Becky entertained Sammy while Matt went outside to look for some firewood. He came back with a big armload and then turned around and went back for some more, as he said that he wanted to gather it before it got dark. When he returned and got the wood stacked where he wanted it, he went back inside and chatted with Becky for a while. He could see that Sammy was getting tired, so he told Becky that they would walk her back to her house since it was getting dark. So they left and walked the short distance back to the Forster house, with Becky carrying back the basket that she had brought over. They said good night, with Becky giving both Sammy and Matt a hug, and then Matt took Sammy back to the cabin and put him to bed. At the Forster house, they also prepared for an early bedtime, as it had been a long day since arriving in Bellevue—but a successful day indeed.

16

Spending Their First Full Day in Bellevue—Wednesday

Matt arose shortly after daybreak and went about getting cleaned up and dressed for the day. He then went outside to get a little firewood to start a fire in the stove to fry some bacon and toast some bread for breakfast for himself and Sammy. When the food was ready, he got Sammy up, and they ate together. Sammy asked if his mommy would be coming back today. Matt said that, no, she had gone on a long journey and probably wouldn't be back for quite a while. Then he got Sammy dressed, and they headed over to the Forsters' at about seven thirty, as Becky was going to watch Sammy while Matt went searching for some kind of work.

The Forster family had also arisen early. The women fixed some breakfast while the men did some work outside in the yard. After they ate, Clint prepared to head to the blacksmith shop. He wanted to be early for his first day of work, which started at 8:00. Ruby had a little more time to prepare for her day, as she didn't need to be at the school until thirty or forty-five minutes after that. They had discussed it with Harvey and decided that Harvey might as well go along with Ruby and at least see what the school had to offer for him.

Clint left for the smithy, and shortly thereafter, Matt arrived at the Forster house with Sammy. He chatted with them for a bit, and Ruby mentioned to him that Daniel Reed would be at the school that day, in case Matt wanted to stop by there and ask him if he had thought of any place where Matt could inquire about work.

Matt left Sammy in Becky's able supervision and went first to the trading post to see what supplies they had in stock. He then went to the hardware dry goods store and talked with Brad and Penny about everything that they kept in stock. He also asked them who was considered to be the town leader in regard to hiring workers, establishing law and order, and doing scouting work such as riding out into the nearby area and looking for any possible problematic people or other things. Brad told him that he might start with the banker, Franklin, or go see Daniel Reed, who had his finger pretty much on the pulse of the town. Or, Brad said, he could talk to Henry at the blacksmith shop. Since he was already in the business area of the town, Matt went to the bank to discuss his thoughts with Franklin, who told him that they had no official law enforcement and no official person who served as a troubleshooter but that Daniel Reed would definitely be a good person to discuss those things with.

It was now approaching ten o'clock, so Matt rode his horse over to the mission building and school that overlooked the river. He just stood there for several minutes, taking in the beauty and might of the river and also noting the many people and boats along the banks and piers. The men were doing various jobs that were no doubt associated with the trading business, the ferrying business, or some kind of a shipping industry.

Matt went inside, asked for Daniel Reed, and was taken to him, at which time Daniel asked one of the other adults to assume command of the instruction for his class. The school had a little over twenty total regular students, who received instruction based on a fairly wide-ranging curriculum. This was a good number of students for a town of 150 people or less, but then the school also took in students from the nearby rural areas. Daniel asked Matt to walk with him to discuss Matt's background and his talents, skills, and abilities. Matt outlined his life and his demonstrated skills, starting with his ability with horses that he had developed in Kentucky, his work with the blacksmith and wagon maker in Louisville, and then his prowess as a scout on the wagon train trail. Daniel listened very intently and then asked about his family, at which point Matt told him the story of Amy and him, their choice to go to Oregon, and the unfortunate event that had claimed her life a few days before. Daniel was very moved by that story and also very impressed with the mental strength of this young man. It took courage, focus, and discipline to be able to deal with such a tragedy yet also be determined to move forward in a positive fashion with his life and the life of his son.

Daniel then started enumerating some of the things that he and other town leaders had been discussing lately. A major discussion had been in regard to the needs they would have as the town's number of residents increased. Main considerations included law enforcement, preservation of the peace, planning for the expansion of the town, repair and renovation of what was already there in the town, and communication with other nearby settlements, and recently they had discussed the turmoil that was heating up in the country due to the issue of slavery. So far, tensions had not reached Bellevue yet, but it seemed like it would only be a matter of time. Other issues Daniel mentioned were the burgeoning shipping industry, utilizing the Missouri River as it went south and then east, agricultural needs, entertainment needs, and religious needs.

Matt absorbed and registered Daniel's words, and he immediately asked Daniel about all the activity presently happening down by the riverbank, particularly if there were any good jobs available down there. Daniel confirmed that those people were either working in the shipping industry, the trapping and fur trade industry, or even the ferrying industry that had been created by Peter Sarpy. Matt also asked if there were any settlers in the area who had horse farms available not only to wagon trains but also to other settlers coming to the area. Daniel replied that, to the best of his knowledge, there was no such person in this immediate area who had that kind of enterprise. Matt thanked Daniel for his time and information and told him that if the town leaders wanted to hire a person for scouting, law enforcement and town security, or anything else that they thought would benefit the town, he would be interested in such a position. He then took his leave and headed down to the area by the river to see what kinds of activities were going on in that location.

Matt located the offices of both the Sarpy Ferrying Company and the Missouri Transport Company, which had started shipping goods both upstream and downstream just a couple of years earlier. Both companies were closely related and had been the brainchildren of Peter Sarpy.

Barges were a main cog of the ferrying company, as they were easier to load and could hold more goods, supplies, and wagons on their main decks. The shipping barges also had holds underneath the deck for the lading of additional materials. The steamboats used by the transport company had ample space for robust amounts of goods and supplies, plus they could travel up and down the river at a fairly good pace. The transport company had a larger number of employees, as it needed not only dock workers but also six or eight men to ride on each steamboat that sailed north or south. Matt talked to the two men who were in charge of each of the operations, and they said that they had a full complement of workers at the time but that they would be very interested in him if something should arise. He gave them his name and told them where he lived, then went on his way.

It was midafternoon when he arrived back at the Forster house, where Becky greeted him warmly. Sammy was still napping, she said, but should be up anytime now. She asked Matt if he was hungry, and he suddenly realized that he was kind of hungry, as he hadn't eaten since breakfast. She prepared a sandwich for him, but she didn't have any French fries. She also gave him a glass of water. He ate the sandwich rather quickly, trying not to be wolfish, but she surreptitiously smiled to herself. She was happy to have been able to make him feel better.

Ruby and Harvey then came home from the school, and after Sammy woke up, they all walked together to another nearby residence. Ruby had been told that day that they could get some eggs and perhaps some fresh vegetables from the family of Ernest and Tillie Gardner, who raised their own chickens as well as having a big garden. Both Matt and Ruby bought some items from the Gardner family. They then walked back to the Forster house, and Matt and Sammy then went on to their own place, carrying their fresh food items. Matt and Sammy had a quiet evening at home and went to bed early as Matt figured that he'd have another long day the next day.

The Blacksmith

$\mathcal{C}$lint had experienced a long day at the smithy as well. He and the blacksmith had tackled a wide variety of projects, on which Clint performed well. They had mended boards of wagons, forged some horseshoes and other items, shoed a couple of horses, repaired some reins, and did a couple of other projects. During the day, Clint and Henry had several discussions about their lives, and Clint discovered that Henry had a wife and three small children and that he lived just a short distance from the smithy. Clint was rather tired as he had worked hard to keep up and to try to impress Henry with his work ethic. But what Clint had found was that Henry was indeed a man with his own impressive work ethic. He looked across the work area at Henry and saw him bent over an anvil with a large and heavy sledgehammer in his right hand, and he was banging away at some metal that he was forging into more horseshoes. Clint kind of chuckled at the scenario and the situation.

His thoughts turned to the poem written in 1840 by Henry Wadsworth Longfellow entitled "The Village Blacksmith." Although written about a blacksmith in Cambridge, Massachusetts, named Dexter Pratt, a neighbor of Longfellow's, everything about the poem (perhaps except the chestnut tree) seemed very appropriate in a comparison to Henry Shorter. Longfellow's blacksmith was depicted as a role model to both youth and older people in the town. He was strong, worked by the sweat of his brow, and did not owe anyone any favors or material. Part of the poem goes like this:

Under a spreading chestnut tree,
The village smithy stands;
The smith a mighty man is he,
With large and sinewy hands;
And the muscles of his brawny arms
Are strong as iron bands.

The poem goes on for seven more pertinent and accurate verses. The final verse summarizes the thought that a hard-working person who is available to the community as a friend is a valuable asset for all people. What made Clint chuckle to himself even more than just the irony of the situation was the fact that the poem author's name was Henry Longfellow and his new boss, who had the brawny arms and sinewy hands, was named Henry Shorter. This all seemed quite coincidental to Clint.

Clint finished up his day at five o'clock but asked Henry if there was anything else that he could do that evening. Henry said no and Clint headed on home, feeling happy about and proud of what he had accomplished on his first day of work. He was so glad that his wife had investigated things in the town and influenced him to stay there and settle down. And he also knew that Ruby was very pleased with the decision and that Becky was tremendously pleased with it. He got home and had some supper with his family, and then they went outside and sat around talking until it began to get dark, at which time they went to bed, knowing that they would have another early day the next day and that it also undoubtedly would be a long day for them all.

Second Full Day in Bellevue–Thursday

The two families started the next day in very much the same manner as the previous day. Matt arrived at the Forster house at about eight o'clock to drop off Sammy. Clint had already gone to work, but the rest of the family and Matt all chatted for a while with Sammy running around, getting into everything. Matt stopped Sammy a couple of times, but he also noticed that Becky went after him on several occasions with a great deal of patience and care. He was impressed with Becky's nurturing of Sammy.

About eight thirty, Ruby and Harvey left for the school, and Matt left to go for a ride out into the surrounding territory to get a look at things. As he rode, his thoughts turned to Amy, and he began remembering all the wonderful times when they had ridden together out in the open air of the Kentucky bluegrass area. He had to stop a couple of times to gather not only his thoughts but also his emotions. Likewise, he wasn't quite sure of exactly what it was that he was checking that day, but he wanted to get a sense of the area, see if there were any good spots to perhaps start a horse farm, and see if there were any dangers to the residents of the town. He wasn't quite sure of what dangers he might be looking for, but perhaps things like pits, quicksand, rattlesnakes, or dastardly villains of various ilk. After riding for a couple of hours, he had not seen any dangers, but he had found a couple of places that looked promising for a horse farm, especially ones that had lots of good grazing areas and also were near water sources. He got off his horse several times in order to more closely examine the texture of the ground and other pertinent land features. Finally, satisfied with what he had found, he headed back toward the town, noting the locations of two or three places where settlers had taken up residence and had built lean-tos for shelter—and not much else. He wondered where the men from those homes went during the day and if they had jobs in or around the town.

Upon returning to town, Matt rode slowly down the main street and noted the locations of the store that sold hardware and dry goods, the bank, the newspaper office, and the post office. When earlier settlers had started to organize the town, they had built a main street that allowed room enough for six separate businesses or enterprises to exist. There was ample space nearby to build many more, if needed. He noticed that only four of the locations were presently being used, so he reasoned that there might be two available for other uses. That set him to thinking about what other uses might be good for the town and how they might align with his own needs for the future.

Since he was already on the main street, Matt went to the newspaper office to see if Daniel might be there, but he found out that Daniel was at the school. Not wanting to bother him at the school again, Matt headed down toward the river, carefully taking in the locations of all the businesses down there, their office locations, which ones had piers or dock areas built, and various other details. He was determined to get a wide range of knowledge of the town and its surrounding area in order to best plan what might be his best future pursuits.

He decided to make his first stop at the office of the company that shipped goods up and down the river. He went in and asked for the owner or manager, after which a rather grizzled gentleman came out to the front area from an office in the back. Matt introduced himself, and the other man identified himself as Roger Lade. They talked a little bit, and Matt discovered that Roger had been a successful fur trapper and had made good money at it. So when the opportunity arose for him to take on this shipping venture, he jumped at it. Roger then told Matt about the advent of the steamboat and how things had advanced to where they were today.

In 1802, Robert Fulton and Robert Livingston had concocted the idea of building a steamboat to ply the Hudson River between New York City and Albany. The resultant boat was named *The Clermont* and first set sail in 1807, traveling 150 miles upstream in about 32 hours and back downstream in about 8 hours. The development of this steamboat had been called Fulton's Folly, but it didn't take long to prove that it was, indeed, not folly but a brilliant idea. Steamboats greatly reduced the time required to travel from place to place, and their usage quickly expanded to other major rivers and their larger tributaries, such as the Ohio, Mississippi, Missouri, and others. The boats operated quite well due to being able to travel in fairly shallow waters, and with their steam power, they could travel upstream against strong currents. In 1810, roughly twenty steamboats were in use, but by the 1830s, there were around twelve hundred.

Steamboats were propelled mainly by steam power, typically driving propellers or paddle wheels, and were used initially in rivers and lakes only. The steamboats used a great deal of wood for their fuel, and the river floodplains and banks were deforested rapidly. This change to the landscape led to a large increase of silt eroding into the riverbeds as the banks became more unstable due to fewer tree roots. The rivers became shallower in places and also a bit wider, and this sometimes caused unpredictable lateral movement of the river channels, which endangered accurate navigation.

Steamboats greatly helped in the development of the economies of the river port cities because moving agricultural and commodity products to markets became easier and quicker. There were many steamboat catastrophes, particularly between 1847 and 1852, which led to the Steamboat Act of 1852. This act placed the steamboats under the jurisdiction of the Department of the Treasury, rather than the Department of Justice, and a procedure for federal maritime inspections was put into place. Nine supervisors were appointed to be responsible for particular geographic areas to make certain that steamboats there followed proper safety procedures. Among the new requirements were hydrostatic testing of the boilers and a steam safety valve installed on all boilers.

Matt asked Roger how often he sent shipments south from Bellevue and how often he sent shipments north. Roger responded that not only were shipments heading out almost every day, both north and south, but that the shipments also carried the mail from Bellevue to the towns north and south on the Missouri. His company make shipments every day strictly from Bellevue, and boats that were taking goods to a location farther up or down the river stopped at his large pier. Matt then asked Roger about the regular sites to which his company sent ships loaded with local goods. Roger named many, including Nebraska City, Brownville, Rulo, and St. Joseph to the south, and Omaha, Fort Calhoun, Tekamah, Decatur, and Sioux City to the north.

Roger explained that the trips, whether to the north or the south, took a full day, but the time depended mainly on which direction they traveled. It was slightly more than a hundred and fifty miles to St. Joseph, and with four stops on the way, the trip normally took only ten hours, give or take an hour, due to the fact that they were heading downstream. Trips to the north to Sioux City were roughly a hundred and ten miles but took twelve hours or more because they were going upstream. Steamboats headed north and south each day and then returned the following day, so Roger had four steamboats for the trips and kept an extra one to be used if repairs were needed on one of the other four.

Matt's final question was in regard to whether Roger's steamboats, or other boats coming into his pier, ever carried horses to other locations. Roger stated that this occurred once in a while and that, most of the time, the horses were coming from either St. Joseph or the Sioux City area. They chatted a while longer, and then Matt left. He decided not to stop at the trading post or at the office of the ferrying company that day. It had already been a long day of riding, so he headed back to the Forster house to pick up Sammy. Ruby and Harvey were just arriving home when Matt got there. He talked with the Forster family for a while, telling them about his travels that day. In return, Ruby also filled him in on what had taken place at the school that day.

Around four o'clock, Matt took Sammy and headed to their log cabin. After he arrived and fed his horse, he and Sammy led the horse a short distance to a place where logs and branches had fallen to the ground due to gusts of wind going through a grove of trees. He chopped up some of the wood to keep at home for firewood and then placed the wood on a pallet attached behind the horse so that the horse could pull it back to their cabin. He and Sammy led the horse back home, and Matt began to unload the firewood and put it away where it would remain dry. Then he got the horse settled for the night in its small, makeshift corral. They then both went inside, and Matt fixed some supper for himself and the boy, although neither was all that hungry.

At about seven thirty, he put Sammy down for the night and then went to sit outside to think about all that had happened over the past couple of years. One of his thoughts turned to the wagon train's stop in Nebraska City. Something turning over in his brain was unsettling to him; it was a statement that he had heard someone—perhaps J. Sterling Morton, if he recalled correctly—make in Nebraska City. He mused on the dimly recalled comment for a while and then gave up his thinking and went inside to bed.

Third Full Day in Bellevue—Friday

he next day, Matt was up early again, tidying up a few things in the cabin and preparing some breakfast for himself and Sammy. As he was preparing for the day, he thought about Becky and all that she had been doing to help him with Sammy. He had settled on an idea to express his appreciation, which he would try to put into effect when he arrived at the Forster house that morning. He and Sammy enjoyed a good breakfast together, and then around eight thirty they headed over to the Forster house. When they arrived, Ruby and Harvey were just leaving for the school.

After they left, Matt told Becky how much he appreciated her help with Sammy. He told her that he wanted to go down to the hardware and dry goods store and let her pick out something that she could use in her everyday life, or just something that she thought was pretty or perhaps even frivolous. Becky argued that he did not need to reward her for her care of Sammy, but Matt insisted that it was the fair thing to do. So she tidied herself up a bit, and they headed to the store to look over the merchandise.

They arrived and were greeted warmly by Brad and a little more stiffly by Penelope. The owners already knew Becky due to the Forster family purchasing the house from them, so they made small talk about how things were going at the house so far. Then, Matt told them that he wanted Becky to pick out something that she wanted and that he would pay for it. He and Sammy went over to the other side of the store while the Pinchers showed Becky their merchandise.

As Matt was looking around in the far corner of the store, he noticed an apparatus that looked like it was some kind of surveyor's instrument. He picked it up and was looking at it when Brad, noticing Matt's interest in that item, came over to tell Matt about it. He said that it was, indeed, a surveyor's instrument. It had been purchased and used by the gentleman who helped lay out the main street for Bellevue years before. When that man had left Bellevue two years ago, he had sold the instrument to Brad, as he had no further use for it. Brad had thought that he would be able to sell it for a profit, but he did not relay that information to Matt. He just stated that he was asking thirty dollars for it and that only twice before had anyone previously showed any interest in it. Brad somewhat knew how the instrument operated, having been given a demonstration by the man who had sold it to him for ten dollars.

By then, Becky had picked out a little music box that she wanted to take home. It played the tune "Oh, Susanna," written by Stephen Foster in the 1840s. She was familiar with the song and felt that it would give her a good feeling when it was playing. Matt paid the Pinchers for the music box, and they put it into a small bag for Becky to carry it out with. Matt, Becky, and Sammy all said goodbye and then headed back to the Forster house.

When they arrived back at the house, Matt was thinking about what he might like to accomplish that day and could not come up with anything. So instead he asked Becky if she would be interested in the three of them going over by the river to enjoy the view and have a little picnic. Sammy clapped his hands with joy, indicating that he thought it was a wonderful idea, and Becky also seemed to be pleased with the thought. So Becky made some sandwiches and packed them along with some fresh vegetables and a jug of water, and they headed for the river.

Becky was quite pleased and excited to be going on this outing with Matt and Sammy. They found a good location overlooking the river, which also provided some shade, and they laid out a blanket where they could sit to enjoy the pleasant scenery. They talked about various things, but as Becky kept glancing at Matt, she could see that he was preoccupied with other things and that his mind was drifting away from the present. She wanted to be closer to him, but she knew that it was way too early for anything more than just being good friends. Matt had a lot of healing to get through. She knew that what was occurring now was all that she could ask for and all that might ever be realized. She did not want to make Matt feel uncomfortable or nervous around her. They continued to talk and think about things and even waved at people on two or three passing boats. Sammy played with a doll that had been brought along and also began playing tag with the trees. He was enjoying the game because he could tag a tree, but it could not then chase him and catch him. Sammy was chortling with joy about his prowess playing tag. They then had their lunch and just laid on the blanket in the shade, enjoying the beautiful day.

Back at the Pinchers' store, Brad and Penny had discussed the recent visit from Matt and Becky, and Penny said she felt that there was some emotional connection between the two young people. Brad disagreed, saying that Matt had seemed quite matter of fact in just wanting to do something nice for a person who had been helping him out. Was Brad correct, or would Penny's women's intuition prevail? Regardless, both Brad and Penny thought that they should consider approaching Becky about helping out at the store from time to time so that they could each enjoy a little time off.

Somewhere around two o'clock in the afternoon, Matt and Becky decided it was time to end the picnic outing and head back to the Forster house. Sammy was okay with heading back, as he could retire undefeated from his game of tag. He had bragging rights for the rest of the day.

They strolled back to the house, stopping and looking at various things along the way. They arrived at the house just before Ruby and Harvey returned from the school. A short time after they got back, Matt brought up their stop in Nebraska City. He asked if anyone remembered some kind of discussion that had taken place at the Morton mansion, Arbor Manor, about land grants. Surprisingly, Harvey perked up, as he had been standing near those having that conversation. He had listened to what J. Sterling Morton was discussing with his old friend, who was part of the wagon train.

Harvey said that Morton had indicated that, over the last couple of years, he had been corresponding with contacts in Washington, DC and that the gist of his comments was that the government had entered into an agreement with the Native Americans a couple of years earlier. Evidently, all the former Native American lands near Bellevue were now owned by the US government, and they wanted to make that land available to any US citizens willing to settle in the Midwest or the far west. But they had not yet determined an exact methodology for doing that.

Matt listened carefully to what Harvey was saying, and all of a sudden the precise thought had been gnawing at his mind for the past couple of days, after looking at that land outside of town, occurred to him. He needed to contact J. Sterling Morton and get some additional information regarding what he had said in Nebraska City just a week or so ago. Matt said his goodbyes to the Forster family for the day and took Sammy home, where Matt would spend the evening drawing up his strategy as to how to proceed.

After careful deliberation as to whether he should ride to Nebraska City to talk to Morton or mail him a letter, he concluded that he should send a letter. After all, he didn't know if Morton would even be in Nebraska City, and riding there seemed more risky than sending a letter. Plus he didn't want to leave Sammy for several days so soon after his mother's death. So Matt put Sammy to bed and then sat down to write a letter of inquiry to Morton. He asked about the status of the former Native American lands and what he needed to do to secure some of that land. He went to bed that night with a plan of action for the next day, to perhaps give him a solid direction for his future in Bellevue.

Letter to J. Sterling Morton and Day-Four Planning—Friday

The next morning, Matt arose early again and went about getting things prepared for the day, including breakfast for Sammy and himself. After they ate and did a few other things to tidy up the cabin, they headed over to the Forster house. He took Sammy over earlier than normal and was able to catch Clint there, too, as he had not yet left for his day at the smithy. He asked Clint to fill him in on how his work at the smithy was going and then asked him what he remembered about that conversation in Nebraska City with Morton. Clint, however, offered no additional help as he had not been involved directly in that conversation. Matt described to everyone what he had in mind. Then Clint stated that he was heading to work, and Matt said that he would ride down to Main Street with him, as he wanted to be at the post office when it opened.

They got down to Main Street and parted ways. Matt entered the post office as soon as it opened at 8:00 and went to talk to Teresa Stamp at the counter. She put the proper postage on the letter to

Morton, and then Matt asked her if the mail had been sent yet to the shipping company for that day's travel down the river. The clerk indicated that they took the mail sacks down to the docking area for the shipping company at nine or nine fifteen and that the ships usually sailed right around ten o'clock. So Matt left the letter with the clerk. He also asked if the post office ever needed any additional help with delivery of mail or other things. Teresa said that those things were all being handled now but that if anything changed, she would contact him. He thanked her and headed on to his next stop.

Matt entered the hardware store and was greeted by Brad, and the two of them had a cup of coffee together and chatted for a bit. Matt said that he was interested in purchasing the surveyor's instrument that he had looked at the day before, but only if Brad had written instructions for it and could show Matt how to operate it properly. Brad went into the back room and came back out with the instruction booklet. Matt looked through it, and his first thought was that it looked like the curriculum for an advanced mechanics class at a university. Brad was also kind of skeptical about the value of the booklet, saying that it looked like it was written in a foreign language or by an overexuberant scientist. Brad said that he would demonstrate for Matt what the original owner had shown him when Brad had bought it from him. He moved the dials on the instrument and manipulated the levers, and the view through the lens came into focus. They could look out the door and down the street, spot something, and then read the gauge to see how far away that object was oriented, along with the latitude and longitude of the location where the object stood. Matt asked if he could borrow the instrument and take it out into the country to see if he could figure out its operation better and if it worked to do what he wanted it to do. He said if it worked properly, he would pay Brad twenty dollars for it. Matt also bought a small notebook to document and keep track of his findings. Brad agreed to the offer on the instrument, so Matt took it and the notebook and left the hardware store. Back inside the store, Penny was already harassing Brad about not getting more money for the instrument. Brad just ignored her since he knew that he would actually be doubling his investment if Matt ended up paying him the twenty dollars.

Matt then rode out into the countryside to the two most favorable locations that he had found the day before. He set up the instrument on its tripod and gradually became more comfortable using it and getting the readings that he wanted. He wrote down the latitude and longitude of the perimeter corners of the areas he thought would be the most favorable. His calculations were that he would be looking to obtain approximately 160 to 200 acres, a bit over what would be a quarter section back in civilized locations such as Kentucky. He then proceeded to take several more readings for other locations in the area, and he carefully recorded all the information in his little notebook. If his plan worked out the way he hoped it would, he would need that additional information for other ventures that he hoped to begin implementing.

He rode back into town, went to the hardware store to pay Brad the twenty dollars, and then took his instrument home. Afterward, he went to pick up Sammy, and he and the Forster family talked about their respective days and what the highlights had been. Ruby invited Matt and Sammy to stay for an early supper, and he thanked her for the offer and accepted. Sammy and Becky were also happy, but she tried not to show it.

After supper, they went back to their cabin, and Matt began thinking about plans for the next day while also trying to entertain Sammy. Once he got Sammy to sleep, he began outlining on a piece of paper from his notebook what he needed to accomplish the next day and which people in the area he needed to talk to about his ideas. He then went outside for a while and looked at the clear skies and the moon and stars. He wondered if Amy was up there looking down at him, too, and trying to watch over him and Sammy. A very nostalgic and powerful feeling swept over him as he gazed upward at the beautiful nighttime sky and thought about how things in this world had been so drastically changed for him. He thought that things were moving into place for him to be able to obtain land to have his desired horse farm, but he knew there were dangers in obtaining land with impenetrable vegetation, excessively hard ground or rocky soil, or unsuitable access to water. He then went back into the cabin and lay down, but sleep would not come for an hour or more. His mind was still racing. Finally, he drifted off to sleep and slept pretty well until morning.

Day Five in Bellevue— Saturday

*M*att arose early again the next day, proceeded to get breakfast ready for himself and Sammy, and prepared the things that he wanted to take with him for the day. Once again, they got over to Forster house before eight o'clock, and he rode alongside Clint as they went down to the main street area. Even though it was Saturday, the downtown businesses were open until at least noon, and sometimes longer. They chatted on the way down to main street and said their goodbyes for the day as they parted near the turnoff to the smithy, which was just around the corner from the south end of the main street. Matt rode on to the newspaper office, figuring that since Daniel did not have school that day, he would be there at the newspaper office working on stories and other information for his weekly newspaper, *The Palladium*.

Matt went into the newspaper office, and Daniel was, indeed, there. His hands were dirty with printer's ink, as he was trying to clean one of his presses. He asked Matt what was on his mind as he kept working on the piece of equipment. Matt outlined what he had been investigating and working on the past few days. Matt's reflections included his ride out into the countryside, his trips down by the river to see the companies that were there, his talks with Lade, his discovery of the surveyor's instrument at the hardware store, his gnawing thoughts about J. Sterling Morton's statements in Nebraska City, and then Harvey's recital of what it was that Morton had been saying. Daniel was eyeing Matt with interest and curiosity. He wondered where Matt's comments were leading, and he said as much. Matt replied that he was pretty sure that, since the Act of 1854 had been passed—in which the government traded to get the rich Native American lands near Bellevue and gave the Native Americans less desirable land tracts elsewhere—settlers were going to be able to obtain this land from the government. He also told Daniel that he had sent a letter to Morton asking him about the act and about whom he could contact back in Washington, DC in regard to purchasing that former Native American land, as well as whether it would be proper at this time to lay a claim to it.

Matt then conveyed that, if it was permissible to claim land and then begin developing it, he would like to set up a small company at one of the vacant stores in town. From his own newfound business, he would help prospective settlers find tracts of land that they wanted to lay claim to and keep records in his office of who was claiming which lands.

Matt would use his surveyor's instrument in doing this work, and he would set a reasonable fee for assisting settlers in the procurement of a property claim. Daniel thought that this was a great idea, and they discussed the vacant stores along Main Street that could be utilized for this venture. Matt would be viewed as kind of a town land clerk and could possibly receive a very small stipend to go along with whatever fees he collected. The banker, Frank Cash, would also have to agree to this idea, but Daniel didn't feel that there would be a problem there. Daniel then cleaned up his hands and told Matt that they could go look at the other vacant stores to give Matt an idea as to which one he might like to utilize.

Daniel grabbed a couple of keys, and they headed to the two vacant store areas. The one just next door to the newspaper office was available and sat very near the middle of the section of buildings. The other open store was the last one on the north end of the street. When they went into each store, Matt looked around, scrutinizing carefully, and he made mental notes of the size of the main area, the size of any back office or storage areas, ventilation and window lighting, and other factors that were less important. Matt told Daniel that he would wait for the response from Morton, and then he would come back to discuss everything again. He thanked Daniel for his time and then headed down toward the trading post, which was about halfway down the hill toward the river, built on a little higher ground so as to avoid the likelihood of possible floods.

Matt entered the trading post and looked around the fairly large supply area, noting that they had furs, blankets, saddles and bridles, clothing, and ammunition, as well as a few guns of various types that matched the ammunition that was available. There were also tents, lanterns, large sections of canvas, and a fairly good supply of various kinds of alcoholic liquor. One corner of the trading post consisted of a small kitchen and dining area that would seat maybe a dozen people. Matt made his way over there and ordered something from the menu to have for lunch. After he was served, he was pleasantly surprised to find that the food was rather tasty. He had been a little worried. He finished eating, looked at a few items of merchandise a bit closer, and then left the trading post.

From there, he headed on down by the river again, this time hoping to talk to the manager of the ferrying operation. He discovered that the manager, Wilbur Ford, had gone for the day, as they had completed the assignments that they had. The office assistant was very talkative and helpful, and Matt was happy to receive the extra information.

Afterward, Matt rode back up to Main Street to find that Clint had already finished working for the day and had headed on home. Matt then followed suit and headed to the Forster house, where he and Sammy enjoyed the remainder of the day with the Forster family. Before heading home to his cabin, Matt discussed the next day with the Forster family, which was a Sunday. They all mutually decided to just spend the day on their own, trying to just be idle and catching up on some necessary relief and relaxation. It was felt that a day of rest was not only prescribed but also earned and needed.

Sunday – A Day of Rest

$\mathcal{T}$he next morning, Matt again rose early, only this time he let Sammy sleep a great deal longer. He got Sammy up at about nine thirty, and they had breakfast. Then Matt decided to take Sammy to the 10:30 church service at the Presbyterian church, which had been built there the year before. Matt had attended church with his family regularly in Kentucky and as a general rule had enjoyed it. He thought it might be good for both of them to have a service to aid them in their emotional healing.

Matt and Sammy walked the short distance to the church, as Matt wondered if the Forster family would be there. They entered the church about ten minutes before service time and looked around, but they did not see the Forster family so they went up the left side of the church about five rows and found enough room for the two of them on the aisle there. The service began, and Matt's mind concentrated on not only the service and the sermon, but he also prayed silently for Amy's soul and for health and happiness for he and Sammy and the Forster family in the future. When the service ended, Matt and Sammy filed out to say their greetings to the preacher, and he noted that the Forster family was ahead of him in the recessional line.

They reached the preacher, Harper Devine, and said a few words to him about how nice the service had been and told him who they were, after which they said "Good day" and went outside. The Forster family was there waiting for them and invited Matt and Sammy over for a Sunday dinner. Matt had hoped to do some silent reflecting that day but reasoned that he could make time to share a meal with them.

Back at the Forster house, they talked for a short while before sitting down to a nice Sunday meal. Many of the food items were things that Ruby had procured from other settlers in the area. They discussed the church service and the preacher. They thought he had done an excellent job with the day's services. Matt asked if anyone knew how long Preacher Devine had been at the church, and Clint filled him in with information he and Ruby had gained at the smithy and at the school.

A reverend named Edmund McKinney and his colleague, J. M. Erwin, had spearheaded the drive to build a new mission when it had become apparent that things were not working well any longer at the old Moses Merrill mission. The new mission building was completed in 1848, with the school and the new church sharing the facility. McKinney made the church into a Presbyterian church in 1850. Daniel Reed and his wife, D. E. Reed, helped McKinney with the operation of the school. McKinney's church followed the principles of the Presbyterian faith, and he remained in that leadership position until 1853, when Reverend William Hamilton took over the running of the church and the school. Hamilton remained in that capacity until 1855. In 1854, the city of Bellevue was incorporated and elected a mayor and some aldermen, and also in 1854 the Kansas-Nebraska Act was passed. Part of that significant act was a trade of Native American land around Bellevue for land to the north near Walthill, Nebraska, along with some land in Iowa. Hamilton was given the option of moving with the Omaha tribe to Walthill, Nebraska, or staying in Bellevue. He went to Walthill. The town leaders began a drive to raise funds for the building of a new church after the incorporation of the town in 1854. When Hamilton departed in 1855, they were without a church leader for a period of time but then were able to hire Harper Devine to take over the services held at the mission. Devine also supervised the final construction of the new church. The new Presbyterian church was usable in 1856 and totally completed in 1858. Hallelujah!

Also, in 1855, Mrs. D.E. Reed, who had been helping at the school, began to operate a school designed more for the increasing numbers of white children, as almost all the Native American children had been moved to other locations. The mission was also used for many other events. In October of 1854, Nebraska's first territorial governor, Francis Burt, was sworn in at the mission building. One reason for his being in Bellevue for that ceremony was that he wished to recommend Bellevue to be the new capital of the Nebraska Territory. Unfortunately, he died two days later. Several residents, thinking that Bellevue's becoming the capital was a sure thing, refused to approve donation of land for the buildings needed.

At that same time, a group of businessmen from nearby Omaha managed to get the capital idea centered on Omaha, a nearby town that was actually just beginning to grow and had fewer amenities than Bellevue. Added to this twist of fate, the new acting governor appointed to replace Burt was T. B. Cuming, and he chose Omaha for the capital, ending Bellevue's opportunity. Omaha remained as the state capital until 1867. On March 1, 1867, Nebraska was admitted to the United States as a state. After the Removal Act was passed in 1830, the capital city was moved farther west, nearer the Platte River and closer to being situated at the center of the state's population. It was placed in the town of Lancaster, whose name was changed to Lincoln later that same year, when the new town was platted. It was named after President Abraham Lincoln. The state capital remains in Lincoln to this day. The new town of Lincoln was officially incorporated on April 1, 1869.

In March of 1855, the first gathering of the Nebraska District Court was held at the mission building. In 1856, the new Fontenelle Bank was opened on the main street of Bellevue, but it went bankrupt not too long after that due to townspeople's panicked withdrawals. It opened again on Main Street in early 1857 under a different name. Townsman and alderman Frank Cash was selected to operate the new bank.

Matt was rather overwhelmed with all this information and asked a couple of questions. He asked Clint if he knew if Daniel Reed was the town mayor. Clint said that he was an alderman but not the mayor. He then said, "You'll never guess who the mayor is."

Matt replied, "Okay, I won't guess, then."

Clint said, "My boss, Henry Shorter, is the mayor."

Matt nearly fainted!

Their next topic for the afternoon focused on the upcoming Fourth of July and whether anybody knew anything about any kind of planned celebration in the town. Many towns and cities across the United States were starting to have some kind of celebration for the day, although it was not made an official national holiday until

1870. Clint had caught wind of only a few festivities from Henry, but they agreed that they should talk to a few folks and try to help get plans organized for the holiday celebration. The Fourth would fall on the following Saturday. Matt and Sammy then went home for the rest of the day and evening.

The Second Week in Bellevue

*M*onday morning dawned bright and clear, and Matt lay in bed thinking about the plans he had outlined for himself for the next couple of days. He dressed for the day and then started preparing breakfast, at the same time centering his thoughts toward a plan of action for the day. He realized that he could not proceed with several of his plans until he heard back from J. Sterling Morton, so a stop at the post office was a necessity. Second, he wanted to take his surveying instrument out into the country and do some additional surveying and plotting of land. Third, he wanted to go to the trading post and meet the owner of that establishment, and fourth, he wanted to go to the blacksmith shop and talk to Henry, now that he knew he was the town's mayor. A couple of other things were also tugging at his thoughts, but they were of lesser importance than those first four.

He woke Sammy about seven thirty and then had their breakfast, while Sammy prattled on about things and in his own way, keeping Matt entertained. They were developing a routine, and it seemed like every day Sammy was a little less sad and a little more excited about the day ahead.

Just after eight o'clock, Matt took Sammy over to the Forster house and chatted with Ruby, Becky, and Harvey until eight thirty, when Ruby and Harvey left for the school, at which time Matt headed down to the main street. His first stop was at the blacksmith shop, where he wanted to talk to Henry. He also asked Clint to listen in since he might be able to add something to the discussion. Matt told Henry about what J. Sterling Morton had said about land being available to settlers following the 1854 Kansas-Nebraska Act, that he had mailed a letter to Morton in Nebraska City about the act the previous Friday, and that he was hopeful he'd get a response either that day or one of the next two days. Matt suggested to Henry that, depending on Morton's response and if it seemed feasible, he then would plan to open a land clerk office on the main street. From his new business, he would start surveying the land outside the town so he could make a listing of properties that might be available to present and incoming settlers. He asked if Henry would have any objection to Matt's claiming one of the spaces on the main street as an office, and Henry said that he would be fine with that idea. Matt also informed Henry that he would be happy to help garner any supplies needed for any Fourth of July celebrations on the upcoming Saturday. He could use his wagon to haul any supplies, if it was needed. Matt then took his leave from the smithy.

He decided that his second stop would be the post office to check on the arrival of the day's mail. He thought that, perhaps, if the boats ran on Sunday, a reply could have come in late Sunday afternoon. When he asked, he was told that boats do not ply the river on Sundays except under unusual circumstances, but sometimes they ran on Saturdays and occasionally a boat arrived late on a Saturday afternoon. Teresa checked for any mail for Matt, but there was none. Matt thanked her and departed for his next stop.

He arrived at the trading post and went inside. On this visit, he asked for the owner. Out from a back office came a man who looked an awful lot like a true mountain man. He had a long, scraggly beard and a deep, four-inch scar on his right cheek, which was somewhat hidden by the beard. The man had a slight limp, but he nonetheless seemed to be an active, vibrant person. Matt introduced himself, and the trading post owner said that his name was Barry Hyde. Matt chuckled a little at that name but then told Barry that he planned to open a land clerk office to help settlers get ownership of land in the area near Bellevue. He asked Barry where he lived and where his workers lived and if he would mind if Matt contacted his employees and him once he got his surveying business up and running. Barry thought that would be a fine idea. They chatted about the upcoming Fourth of July weekend, and Barry invited Matt to return to his building on Saturday for a special barbecue meal and perhaps a libation or two. Matt said that he would plan to attend, and they said *adios* for the day. (Both had learned some Spanish along the way.)

Matt's only remaining task for that day was exploring the countryside and conducting some additional surveying, but he began thinking that this activity might be putting the cart before the horse because his project might get scrapped by the return information from Morton. So he instead went to the Sarpy Ferrying building and asked for the manager. The manager turned out to be Peter Sarpy's son-in-law, Wilbur Ford, who was usually called Will. Matt told him who he was, that he had been in town for only a week, and that he just wanted to familiarize himself with the local businesses and their owners and managers. Ford was very gracious and even gave Matt a kind of sketch of the successful life of his father-in-law. They shook hands again and said that maybe they'd see each other on the upcoming holiday. Matt departed the office building and started heading back to the Forster house. He rode back slowly, meandering a bit up some unpaved and rutted side streets. He made note of some of the more unique structures and decided that he needed to add a town map to his notebook, should he be able to begin his tasks as a city clerk.

He arrived at the Forster house about two thirty, just as Brad Penny, the hardware owner, was mounting his horse and starting to head back to the main street. Brad stopped for a moment and chatted with Matt, telling him that he had been asking Becky if she might be interested in working part-time for him. Brad then headed on toward the main street, and Matt went into the house. He waited about ten minutes for Becky to bring up Brad's visit, but she did not, so Matt brought it up. She said that Brad had offered her some part-time work but that she had told him she needed to think about it. Her hesitation was mainly because she enjoyed her time with Sammy so much and that she felt obligated to keep watching him, but she hadn't told Brad that information. She looked at Matt with a look that was almost forlorn and also kind of guilty.

Matt said, "You have been a very special person to Sammy and have gone out of your way to take care of him and protect him, but if you need to do some part-time work, you should do so." He also indicated that some other arrangements could be made if it became necessary. He was very understanding of Becky's dilemma and of her confused state at the moment. She listened to him, smiled, and said, "Thanks for your understanding words and for your concern about me." At that point, Ruby and Harvey arrived home from the school and, after everyone chatted for fifteen or twenty minutes, Matt took Sammy and headed to their cabin.

The next morning, it was kind of a cool day, and rain seemed to be on the horizon. The rain started in earnest just about the time that Matt arrived at the Forster house with Sammy. Due to the precipitation, he remained inside talking to Becky while waiting for the downpour to diminish somewhat. She said that she had discussed Brad's offer with her parents the night before and that they had told her to go ahead and get some part-time work if she could. They would work out the details of watching over Sammy if and when that was still needed. Harvey could take the day off from school if it became necessary for him to watch Sammy, or they would figure out an alternative plan. Matt told Becky that he would stay at her house with Sammy if she wanted to go down to the hardware store and work out details with Brad and Penny. She agreed that a trip there would be a good idea so that she could accept the offer.

They continued talking until the rain subsided, and then she rode Matt's horse down to Main Street. He had offered his horse so that she wouldn't have to saddle her own or risk getting caught in more rain.

Almost an hour later, Becky returned and said that she had been hired to work one day a week, plus one evening, as the Pinchers had recently started staying open on Tuesday and Thursday evenings until 8:00 in order to get more business from those people who were working longer summer hours. Matt then announced that he had a couple more stops to make but that he would be back earlier than normal to pick up Sammy that afternoon. He headed out to the post office to check on the mail that had come in on the boat late the previous afternoon.

He entered the post office, and Teresa was behind the counter sorting the day's mail that had arrived. Immediately, she smiled at him and told him that there was a letter for him. She handed it to him, and he glanced at the return address on the envelope—it was, indeed, from J. Sterling Morton. Morton must have sat down immediately after receiving Matt's letter and composed a return letter. Matt thanked Teresa and took the letter outside and down to a spot in front of the vacant building he was interested in for his office.

He opened the letter and read it with a great deal of interest and then excitement. Morton had outlined the procedures that would be necessary for settlers to obtain land but also said that even though these guidelines had not yet been officially adopted by the federal government, they were allowing settlers to begin the process of obtaining land ownership. He cited his discussions and correspondence with his contacts in Washington, DC, in particular with Robert McClelland, who had been secretary of the interior from 1853 until just this past March, and also with the new secretary of the interior, Jacob Thompson, who was serving under the new president of the United States, James Buchanan. Morton, himself, had recently been appointed as secretary of the Nebraska Territory, which also made him a very valuable contact and asset to Matt.

The Department of the Interior had been created in March of 1849. Prior to that date, its business had been handled by the State Department. The Mexican War from 1846 to 1848 had further prompted the proposal for a new department since the responsibilities of the federal government were growing rapidly. Secretary of the Treasury Robert Walker championed the idea of a new department, citing the need to move several departments— the General Land Office, the Department of Indian Affairs, Land and Resource Management, Wildlife Conservation, Territorial Affairs, the National Park Service, 544 national wildlife refuges through the Fish and Wildlife Services, and the Patent Office—into one unified federal department. A bill authorizing the creation of the new department passed the US House of Representatives on February 15, 1849, and then spent over two weeks in the Senate (some things never change). The bill passed the Senate narrowly, and the department was officially created on March 3, 1849, the night before the inauguration of the new president of the United States, Zachary Taylor.

The Donation Land Claim Act of 1850 developed from there, which aided Matt in his endeavors. Settlers could begin claiming land in former Native American areas, as well as in Oregon and other places throughout the West. Any US citizen could apply for public land in the allotted areas. Usually, claims were for 160 acres but could be up to 320 acres. In Oregon, people could apply for up to 640 acres. The applicant had to be willing to settle on and farm the land. There was a three-step procedure, which included (1) filing an application; (2) improving the land; and (3) filing for the patent (deed) to the land. The applicant needed to not only reside on the land for five years but also show improvements to the land, with that process and verification being completed within seven years. There was a small filing fee of ten dollars for the smaller properties and eighteen dollars for larger properties in order to temporarily hold a claim to the land.

This procedure was designed to be augmented and replaced by

passing the Homestead Act, but that legislation kept getting delayed, so the act passed in 1850 was kept on the books and used for the ensuing twelve years. In 1860, the Homestead Act was finally voted on, but it failed to pass. In that act, the government was offering the land for twenty-five cents an acre. Its proponents kept pushing it, and on May 20, 1862, the Homestead Act was officially passed and signed into law by President Abraham Lincoln.

So, in essence, the framework for Matt's plan was not only there but had been put into action, pending changes that might come from the passage of the Homestead Act in later years. The government wanted to encourage the project and give incentives to settlers who took advantage of the plan. Morton gave Matt the names and addresses of two people in Washington, DC to whom he should send his application. Alternatively, he could send it to Morton himself and he would forward it, or Matt could check with the highest administrator of the Nebraska Territory on it, but Morton felt it would be best to get the application sent to Washington along with a request for any future mailing addresses for later applications.

Matt then rode back to the Forster house, discussed his plan, and then took Sammy and went back to their cabin so that he could spend the evening laying out his plans for the next day. He was quite excited about the opportunities that now lay ahead for him.

At home that evening, after he had fixed supper for Sammy and himself, he spent some time playing with Sammy while also mentally formulating the best procedure for moving ahead with his plans. After putting Sammy down for the night, Matt took out his notebook, jotted down his many thoughts, and outlined his procedure for getting to where he wanted to be.

The next day was Wednesday, and after going through their usual routine, Matt took Sammy over to the Forster house before eight o'clock as he wanted to talk to Clint alone, possibly riding down to Main Street with him to do so. On their way down to the smithy, Matt broached the subject of land possibilities with Clint in order to ascertain whether Clint would like to apply for some of the land available outside of town. He stated that this moment provided an excellent opportunity for Clint to obtain an application for land that was available and also to possibly try to reserve some additional land for Harvey, who was now approaching seventeen years of age and might want to have some land of his own for the future. Clint actually had already given some thought to looking toward a land purchase, so it didn't take much to convince him. He hadn't thought about getting land for Harvey, too, but thought that it was also a good idea. Matt told him that he'd be out surveying the remainder of the day and that he would complete the applications and get them mailed either the next day or Friday. Clint asked if any money was needed, and Matt told him that he would take care of it and that Clint could reimburse him later.

Clint then went to work at the smithy, and Matt went to the newspaper office to procure a space on the main street from Daniel. Then, he went to the hardware store and purchased a desk, several chairs, a couple of lanterns, and a few other items and got them moved over into his new office space, which happened to be right next door to the hardware store. After that, Matt rode home to get his surveying equipment and his notebook, and he headed out to the countryside to accelerate his surveying work.

He spent the day doing surveying and recording measurements into his notebook, along with driving stakes into the ground at the various corners of properties that he was platting. He rode around for a while, looking for any water that was available in the area, before he started finalizing his plan for determining property boundaries for the various plats. A couple of creeks ran through the area, one of which later became known as Papillion Creek. He figured that with those two creeks, there was probably a pretty good water table underground that would provide water for a large majority of the land that was available.

Around four o'clock, Matt rode back into town, picked up Sammy, and went home for the evening, where they ate supper, as usual. Then, Matt spent time putting his notations and measurements down into his notebook in a more professional manner. Sammy played quietly with his toys and fell asleep on the floor. Matt put him to bed, then prepared the land applications for himself and for Clint, and got them ready for mailing the next day. Matt then went outside for a while to look at the sky and the stars and think about the mysteries of life.

Thursday, Matt went to the post office after dropping off Sammy and mailed the application letters to both J. Sterling Morton and the secretary of the interior in Washington, DC. Just for special emphasis, he also sent one to the president of the United States, James Buchanan. He figured it couldn't hurt.

Matt spent the remainder of that day and also the next day surveying the land available in the surrounding area and recording its locations, dimensions, measurements, and other pertinent information into his notebook. By the middle of Friday afternoon, he was quite pleased with the progress that he had made but also quite exhausted from all his activity and the tensions that came with embarking on this very necessary project. He went back into town and stopped to see Daniel to tell him that everything was now in motion, and Daniel informed him that the town council had approved Matt to be paid by the town for his work.

Matt then went to pick up Sammy and accepted an invitation to stay for supper with the Forsters. He told them about his progress with the recording of land, and then they all discussed what they would do the next day to assist with the Fourth of July celebration. Matt took Sammy home, and they played together for a while and then both went to bed, the end of a long, arduous, and productive week.

24

The Fourth of July and the Incident

Matt awoke on July Fourth at his usual early time but let Sammy sleep late. Matt went for a short walk around the neighborhood, while keeping an eye on his cabin, to see if anything was getting organized as of yet. He didn't see anything that told him much, so went back to the cabin and started preparing some breakfast. He considered having raw meat, plain white bread, and some blueberries for breakfast (so that it would be red, white, and blue) but decided against it because Sammy really liked his bread put on the stove and browned a bit, and he probably wouldn't eat raw meat. So Matt cooked some bacon, browned some bread, and prepared small bowls of blueberries, then he woke Sammy up and brought him to the breakfast table.

Matt and the Forster family had agreed to meet about eleven o'clock near the blacksmith shop, as there was to be a cookout near there for the residents of the town and those of the surrounding area. Various factions of the community donated most of the food, but people partaking in the cookout event were asked to also make a cash donation, which would go to the township fund for use in projects that might later come up in the town. They were thinking about putting up streetlights on Main Street, but many of the town aldermen thought that they should wait until electricity had been invented, which happened in 1879, when Thomas Edison got the bright idea to make lighting for houses and eventually got his light bulb to work satisfactorily. (Some people wonder if Edison was the great-great-great-grandfather of Debby Boone, who recorded "You Light Up My Life" in 1977.)

At eleven o'clock, Matt and Sammy arrived at the cookout area and found that the Forster family was already there. First, they all looked at the various displays and then at what was available at the food tables. Of course, there were hot dogs and baked beans and apple pie, but there were also other kinds of pie, a few cakes, some sweet corn, and some hamburgers, with sliced cheese and sliced tomatoes available. Other odds and ends rounded out the menu, such as condiments, pudding, lemonade, and sliced bread. A libation table was set up nearby for people to purchase various whiskey drinks. For beer, they had to go to the trading post, which had a keg on tap. They all then went through the line to fill their plates, donated to the town cause, and then found a place to sit down and have their lunch. Ruby had brought along a couple of blankets, which they spread on the ground and sat down upon. Matt inspected Sammy's plate and discovered a pickle, a slice of cheese, a hot dog with no bun, and two pieces of pie—one apple and one cherry. Matt said to Sammy, "What, no cake?" They all greatly enjoyed their meal and had a lively conversation. They were interrupted a few times by other attendees who came by to say hello to them, with some of them needing to introduce themselves.

They lounged around that area for another hour or so, just talking and enjoying one another's company as well as the banter of other people who were in attendance. Since they were right next door, Clint took them all to the blacksmith shop and showed them around. It was quite an impressive and well-organized shop, and Clint was proud to be a part of it. Then, Matt took them to the building where his new office was located. He showed them the spartan furniture arrangement and outlined his plans for getting the place organized in the future. He also pointed out that his office was right next door to the hardware store so, if Becky was ever working at the hardware store, she could check to see if he and Sammy were in his office and come in to visit with them. Becky said, "I wouldn't need to be working at the hardware store in order to come in here and visit you." Ruby glanced at both Becky and Matt and thought, *Those two are thinking about different meanings.*

After dawdling around for a while longer, they headed down toward the trading post at about two o'clock. As they approached the trading post, they could see a line of twenty or thirty people down by the pier, near where the ferries docked. Clint asked someone what that line was for, and he was told that the ferry company was offering free river rides for people that day. As they looked more closely in that direction, they could see a ferry just then returning to shore. So they quickly discussed taking a ride and were unanimous in their decision to go down and get in line. They hurried down to the pier and got in line, unsure how many people could get onto the ferry each time. As the riders on the ferry just returning came off, they could see that it held quite a large number of people. Even though about ten or twelve people who had been on the prior cruise stayed on, the two families made it onto the next excursion, with five or six more still coming on after them.

The ferry pulled away from shore and headed up the river toward Omaha. One of the ferry employees began narrating for the benefit of the passengers. He said the trip to Omaha was about eight miles and normally took a half hour or more. He added that they would not be going all the way to Omaha but instead would head across the river to the Iowa side, come back down the river to their ferry station there, then cross the river back to their Bellevue station. The trip would take about an hour total. He also said that if they wanted to take a cruise of the same time length to the south (down river), they could stay on for the next cruise and do so. They had ridden for almost a half hour when the narrator pointed out up ahead a landmark or two on the Nebraska side of the river. He said those landmarks showed where Omaha was located. The ferry then turned and went across the Missouri to the Iowa side, where he again pointed out a couple of landmarks to the north showing where Council Bluffs was located. The ferry then cruised along the Iowa side, only taking about twenty minutes to reach their station on the Iowa side of the river. They waved at some workers who were on the dock there, and then the ferry turned west and headed back across the Missouri to the Bellevue dock.

As they were cruising, Matt had been thinking about the ensuing cruise that would head south. He thought that it might come close to the confluence of the Platte and the Missouri, and he didn't really want to see that location again as of this moment. Memories of Amy's death began flooding his consciousness. As it turned out, Ruby also had been thinking about the tragedy, and she said that she thought they should get off in Bellevue and enjoy the local festivities. After all, they could get a boat ride just about any time if they really wanted one. Matt was happy to agree with her. When they got off the ferry at the dock, it was approaching four o'clock in the afternoon.

Next, they wandered around the dock area for a while, then went up toward the barbecue that was taking place just outside the trading post. A fairly large crowd was gathered near the barbecue, and it was getting rather loud, with many people feeling boisterous. This revelry was due in no small part to the liquor and beer being served. Many of the settlers and townspeople had been at the event since morning, and a lot of them had now been at the area near the trading post for several hours.

The folks who had been drinking since morning were beginning to feel no pain and a great deal less inhibited. Matt and the Forster family decided to go ahead and get their supper a little early so that they could get away from this rather raucous location. They paid, got their meal tickets, and then went through the line to get their food and beverages. There wasn't much of anywhere to sit, so they again spread the blankets Ruby had brought and sat down to eat. They were enjoying their meal and having a nice conversation. As they were getting close to finishing their meal, Sammy spilled his drink, and Becky quickly volunteered to go get another one for him. She walked across to the table where the drinks and water were and asked for another lemonade.

Unbeknownst to Becky and the rest of her group, a rather inebriated man had been watching her closely for the past half hour or so. In fact, leering might be a better description. This man walked up to her at the drink table, said that his name was Les Manners, and told her he thought she was the prettiest girl at the event. He asked her what her name was. She didn't know what to think or how to respond, so she didn't say anything except, "I'm sorry. I don't know you, and I have to get back to the people I'm with." Then Les grabbed her arm and told her that she needed to be more friendly, not try to dismiss him in such a rude manner. She tried to pull away, but he only gripped her arm tighter and continued to say demeaning things to her.

Meanwhile, Harvey had been watching what was going on, and he got up and walked over to where Becky and the man were struggling. Harvey told the man to let go of her right then. Les did not let go, but he did turn and stare at Harvey to size him up a little. He let go of Becky and took a swing at Harvey. Harvey was ready for this sort of sneak attack, and he ducked away from the swing, then immediately came up behind the man and got him into a bear hug. Les began flailing and kicking, but Harvey was a very strong young man and did not relax his grip.

By then, Matt and Clint had also arrived at the scene, and they both told the man to quit struggling or they would also enter the fray. The man did stop resisting but continued glaring at them. Clint asked what had happened, so Harvey told him what he had seen and done. Clint asked Les what he had been doing and whether what Harvey said was true. The man just glared at them all. Clint said, "I'm going to ask my son to let you go, and then I want you to immediately leave here and go home."

Les muttered something vulgar, which caused Harvey to increase the pressure he was exerting against the man's arms and shoulders. Finally, Les groaned and said, "Okay, I'll leave."

Clint said, "I'm going to ask my son to release you, and you'd better do what you agreed to and leave here right now or it will get worse for you."

Les said okay, and Clint told Harvey to release him. After being released, Les stretched his sore arms and shoulders and then glared at them all. He said, "You ain't heard the last of this yet." He then turned and stomped and stumbled his way up the hill to where his horse was, clumsily mounted his horse, and rode away, weaving in the saddle as the horse headed onto the riding path.

Clint turned to the crowd that had gathered and asked them if they knew who the man was and where he lived. Someone spoke up and said that the man was not from here; he was in town to sell some furs and trade for goods and would undoubtedly be leaving town soon. They also said that the man had been rather mean and obnoxious the entire afternoon. The men then went back to where Ruby and Becky were now folding up the blankets. Matt touched Becky's shoulder and asked her if she was okay. She replied that she was fine and thanked him for his concern, but it was obvious that she was still shaken by the events. They all left to head back home.

On the way home, Clint and Matt agreed that, for the next few days, they would ask around about the man and double check to make certain he was gone. They arrived at Matt's cabin first, and then the Forster family headed on to their own house. As they settled down for the evening, they thought about all the good things that had happened that day and how they hadn't expected it to end with the kind of fireworks that had broken out.

The Rest of the Summer

*O*n July 5, Matt and Clint rode around town and its adjacent area, checking on the whereabouts of the spurious thug from the holiday celebration, Les Manners. They talked to several men in town and in areas near town and were assured by all that, if any of them saw the man, they would let Matt or Clint know about it. After a few days with no reports of the man still being around, they were satisfied that he indeed had left the area.

During that first full week of July, Matt received documentation that their applications had been verified and approved by Washington, pending a later official act authenticating land grants. Matt and Clint discussed the applications and how to proceed with their newly acquired land. They both felt that they should plan for some minimal improvements in order to satisfy the requirements for living on the land. Since Matt had already installed stakes outlining the borders of their properties, they felt that the first thing they should do was to erect some kind of visible structures that they could use for storage, perhaps later expanding the structures and making them into their homes.

So they drew up plans for storage structures on all three properties, calculated what quantity of wood and roofing and even windows that they would need, and then ordered it all through the hardware store. Brad had enough wood supply on hand to get them started, but he had to place a special order to replenish his own stock and also to complete their order. First, Matt and Clint decided on the best locations to put the structures on each property. Since all three properties were very close to one another, it didn't really matter which one they completed first, but they decided to do Matt's first because he would be out there more often due to his surveying and record keeping. It made the most sense for him to be able to also do some work on the storage structures while he was out there.

On Wednesday, July 8, Matt took Harvey with him out to his property. They identified the preferred location on Matt's property for a structure and immediately dug holes for its four corner posts and two center posts, one near the middle of each side of the planned frame of the structure. In the middle of the two sides that would have doors or windows, they then dug holes for center beams as well as a hole for a center beam directly in the middle of the structure. These three beams would then be connected to one another across the top of the structure by two-by-four boards with others running from the center beams down to the four corner posts, forming a frame onto which they could then nail the roof boards themselves. The actual roof would be made up of two-by-twelve boards, with a weatherproofing material under them.

The next day, Clint took the day off, as did Harvey. At seven o'clock in the morning, the three of them loaded up one of the wagons with the corner posts, wood slats, and roofing they already had, along with nails and hammers, spades, shovels, ladders, and other tools, and they went out to Matt's property. They put the posts into the ground and filled in the holes with some nearby stones, combined with the dirt they had just dug out the day before. Their next task was to nail on the top crossing boards of the structure, from corner post to center post to corner post and so on. These crossing boards were two-by-four boards, giving their structure immediately improved stability. They decided on the best locations for door frames and windows, and they carefully framed those areas with precise and deliberate calculations and measurements. Then they got the three center beams set and the dirt filled back in, and they focused on the diagonal support boards from the center beams down to the corner posts and the center posts. Once those steps were completed, they took a break around two thirty to eat lunch and to quench their thirst.

After their lunch break, they sealed the roof sections with tar paper–like materials they had brought to help seal out the elements. They then started installing the roof boards that they had brought with them, which were three times wider than the crossing boards. They knew that this task would take them the rest of the day, as they not only would be working from ladders but would have to saw the ends of every board to fit the edge of the roof structure they had already put in. Matt and Clint spent the entire afternoon on the ladders doing the sawing and nailing, while Harvey carried the materials to them.

It was well after six thirty when they completed the roof boards. Doing the bottom roof boards was quite easy, but as they got higher up the roof and had to climb onto the roof itself to do their nailing and sawing, they had to be extremely careful so as not to slide off the roof or accidentally split any boards. They finished their work for the day, and as they stood there admiring what they had accomplished, Matt said, "I feel a little bit like Julius Caesar."

Clint and Harvey asked him what he meant.

He said, "I came, I sawed, I conquered." They all laughed.

Clint then said, "Do you plan to plant corn here?"

They loaded up their stuff and went back to town, feeling a big sense of accomplishment.

The following Saturday, Matt and Harvey went back out and began placing floorboards and nailing up the siding boards. Clint worked at the smithy until noon and then came out to help. Matt and Harvey had finished putting in the wooden floor of the structure and had just finished the first side wall on the structure when Clint arrived. With the additional help of a third person to hold the waterproofing sections and the siding boards in place while the other two nailed, finishing up the other three sides did not take too long, except around the door frame and the window frames.

They then installed coverings over the windows and put the door into place, attaching it properly to the frame using hinges. They also drilled holes for the lock and deadbolt mechanisms and put the door into place. They then tried out the key, and it worked precisely as it should. It had been another successful day of work. From then on, they could store any new materials for use on the other two properties inside of this structure and keep it locked up and secure.

For the next two months, as their supply orders came in at the hardware store, they got together a few times to work on the other two structures. Clint had asked Henry if he could have the next four Mondays off so they could work at their properties, and Henry granted him that request. Harvey decided to discontinue school altogether for the summer so that he would always be available to help Matt or to work on Mondays with his dad and with Matt. School only was to be in session until the end of July anyway before it took a two-month break.

For the following two Mondays, July 13 and 20, the rest of their supplies had not yet arrived at the hardware store so they worked on other things on the properties. They picked out a strategic place on Clint's property and began the process of drilling a well. They dug deep down into the earth in a place that seemed likely to have water, and eventually they got water to come out. They then installed a pump at the ground level and applied the proper mechanism to regulate the water flow. Having water readily available on the property would be invaluable in helping them succeed with their future agricultural plans.

This process took the better part of that first Monday. On the second Monday, they did the same on Matt's property and again succeeded, this time in fewer than six hours. They were making good progress with their planning and renovations. Matt and Harvey also completed work on other things on other days. On some days, Harvey even helped Matt with the surveying. The two of them also completed some needed caulking on the roof of the structure they had built on Matt's property.

On July 23, the remainder of their building supplies arrived at the hardware store, so on the following Monday, July 27, they began the construction of the building structure on Clint's property. Matt and Harvey had been there on the previous Friday and Saturday, digging the holes for the corner posts, center posts, and center beam. They began installing the beams about seven thirty in the morning and again worked all day, up until early evening, to complete all the work on Clint's structure, including caulking of the roof seams.

The following Monday, August 4, the structure on Harvey's property went up. They built it only after Matt and Harvey had worked on completing an operational well during the week and then digging the holes for the posts and beam on Friday. They started on Harvey's structure at about eight o'clock in the morning and finished up around six thirty that evening. For the time, they were pretty much done for that year with their land improvements, except that Matt still wanted to start building a perimeter fence on his property. Much progress had been made on the improvements to their properties. Matt had dutifully recorded everything completed so far for when he needed to send a progress report to Morton and to Washington, DC.

Also during this time, Matt had continued to survey all the other nearby available land and to break it up into plots for aspiring settlers. As of August 1, he had measured, surveyed, and platted twenty-eight properties, with six applications from new settlers already being approved. This, in itself, would bring him an additional one hundred fifty dollars, with each new application approval costing the applicant twenty-five dollars.

Becky had started working part-time at the hardware store in the last couple of days of June. She worked on Tuesdays from 9:00 a.m. to 5:00 p.m. and also on Thursday evenings from 2:00 p.m. to 8:30

p.m. On Tuesdays, Harvey stayed home and watched Sammy, or Matt simply took him with him to work for the day. On Thursdays, Harvey also filled in for Becky at 2:00 or Ruby came home from the school early if need be. Becky continued to take charge of Sammy on all the other weekdays and sometimes on weekends as well if Matt had something really pressing to get done. On the Tuesdays that Becky worked, she would eat lunch at the store unless Matt happened to be in his office that day. If he was, she would go next door to eat lunch with him. On some of those days, Matt also had Sammy there for the day. Becky continued to be an invaluable aid to Matt, even as she tried to maintain the appearance that she was not too interested in him, although she definitely was.

Clint continued working at the smithy except for the four Mondays that he had asked to have off. There was still plenty of work for both he and Harvey as more and more settlers arrived in town. Many settlers needed new shoes for their horses, saddle repairs, wagon repairs, or some other task. Clint and Henry were both very skilled, and their customers were almost always extremely pleased with the quality of work that they received from them.

Ruby continued her work at the school even though Harvey had decided not to continue through the month of July, as he had too many other things to do. The number of students in the school was continuing to increase, as more and more settlers arrived in the town and decided to settle down there. Ruby was pleased to be an educator at the school and very happy with the leadership of Daniel and his wife, D. E. Classes at the school would continue until Friday, July 21, and then not be in session for at least two months.

As stated previously, Harvey, who had been helping at the school in June, decided to not go there in July, as he had agreed to watch Sammy on Tuesdays and possibly on Thursday afternoons, and he was also needed to help with the properties they had recently acquired through their land applications. He was becoming not only stronger but also even more of a responsible person than he had been previously.

August arrived, and things continued for everyone much as they had in July except for Ruby, who now had a lot more time on her hands. After consulting with both Clint and Matt, Ruby spent a lot of her time in August making curtains and other amenities for the new structures on their rural properties. She also watched Sammy now on Tuesdays and on Thursday afternoons so that Harvey could be free for his work out on the properties and also for helping out other farmers and settlers.

Matt alternated his days between n the properties, measuring more plots of land, removing brush out on their properties, building a drinking trough for each property, and starting to put up sections of a wooden-posted perimeter fence around his property. He knew that he eventually wanted to bring some horses there and start a horse farm, so he needed a corral. Harvey helped him with this property work several days a week. On other days, Matt worked in town at his office, both drafting correspondence and recording land applications and deeds. He also helped new settlers develop their properties when he had time to do so.

About mid-August, a letter came for Matt from his mother in Kentucky. He had not heard anything from her or his father in more than a year. In fact, a word had not passed between them since long before he and Amy had begun thinking about heading west. His mother, Susan, acknowledged the letter that Matt had sent them back in early June, thanked him for sending that information, and expressed her condolences at the loss of Amy. She also noted that she had gone over to the Hughes' horse ranch and expressed her condolences to their long-standing enemy. She said that she had also had urged them to set aside any past differences with her husband or with Matt and Amy and to try to come together in order to someday be able to meet and support their mutual grandson.

She expressed that Amy's parents, Jasper and Caroline, had been hit hard by the news about Amy, and it was still weighing heavily on them. They had said they would give the matter some thought and thanked Matt's mother for coming over. His mother also said she then had a serious conversation with Matt's father, Benjamin, and that he himself was beginning to mellow a little. A large part of that was because he would eventually like to know and be close with his grandson. She closed her letter by telling Matt that they were both in good health, as were his two sisters, and that she hoped they could maintain a correspondence and eventually arrange a visit to Bellevue, or perhaps he could arrange a visit back to Kentucky.

Matt sat down that same night and began composing a long letter to his parents to tell them about everything that had happened since they arrived in Bellevue, about his job as a recording clerk, and about his plans for the future.

26

The First Winter in the Heartland

*S*eptember passed by with lots of continuing activities that involved the Forster family and Matt and Sammy. Work continued at the smithy for Clint, while Matt continued his surveying, platting, and recording and approving of land applications, and he also kept helping new settlers develop their properties. One man he helped quite a bit and got to be good friends with was Claude Buster. Ruby continued making things for their new homes and repairing things at the house, while Becky continued her part-time job and also watching Sammy at least four days each week. Harvey continued working on the properties, doing things to help neighbors and other settlers get situated on their land, and watching Sammy when needed.

October arrived, and the days began to get a bit cooler and the trees began changing colors. It was a beautiful time of year in Bellevue. Everyone greatly enjoyed the milder weather and the panorama of scenery that went along with the changing colors. Many trees were dropping their leaves, and breezes often kicked up swirls of leaves that flew in every direction.

Matt took full advantage of the beautiful weather to do more surveying and finish up his perimeter fencing on his country property, as well as some additional fencing for a corral. Just before the middle of October, Matt received another letter from his mother. It didn't add much to her first one except to reiterate that both she and Matt's father would now like to arrange for them all to get together and to ask Matt what his thoughts were on the matter. She wished Matt and Sammy a happy Thanksgiving and a merry Christmas.

Matt pondered all this for a couple of days and then sent a reply to his parents. He said that he was glad they were well and that he and Sammy were also doing very well. He told them that he would not be able to come visit next year because his surveying business would be in full swing by then. He needed to remain in Bellevue to help settlers and keep up with the filing of applications and other documents. He also had his new property to make improvements on, and he informed them of his idea to purchase some horses and start a horse farm so he could make horses available to the new settlers who arrived, if they needed any. He went on to invite them to come to Bellevue to visit in the spring or summer and to see all the happenings going on in this frontier town.

The next day, he mailed the letter after adding a few more tidbits and anecdotes to his message. He also added his wishes to them for a nice holiday season and for a mild winter. After sending the letter on its way, he went over to his office and worked on documents for the remainder of the day.

In November, the weather got chillier, and flurries of snow appeared a couple of times. Matt, Sammy, and the Forster family got together for a very festive Thanksgiving at the Forster house. They had obtained a turkey and some potatoes from the Gardner family, and Ruby and Becky had made some pies as well as some other side dishes in addition to the potatoes and gravy. They talked a lot, played some games, and went for a walk to work off some of the food. They all said their thanks for a successful first five and a half months in Bellevue and prayed for a good ending to the year and for a bright, happy, and successful 1858.

The second week of December was marked with heavy snow. It also turned extremely cold during that time. The families were using lots of firewood to stay warm, so when the weather warmed up some around the middle of the month, the men set out with a wagon and some saws to get as much firewood as they could load into the wagon. One might say they had a burning desire for firewood. It took about a half a day, but they did get the wagon filled up, returned to Matt's cabin and unloaded not quite half of it, then went on to the Forster house and unloaded the rest.

Christmas came, and they all attended a delightful Christmas Eve church service administered extremely well by Preacher Devine. They sang many Christmas songs and harkened to the positive message about the birth of Jesus, which Sammy actually listened to quite attentively. Afterward, he had several questions for his dad about the holy events described by the preacher.

The next day, they all got together at the Forster house again and had a very merry Christmas. Matt and Sammy arrived there early carrying a big bag of gifts. They camped out in the main living area, talked, and enjoyed hot coffee and juice and some rolls that Ruby had made. They exchanged gifts and took turns opening them. Had he been allowed to do so, Sammy would have had all his gifts torn open before the others even started lifting ribbons from their packages. Instead, they all came up with a plan of going around the room in a round-robin fashion in order of their ages. So, Sammy went first, then Harvey, then Becky, then Matt, then Ruby, and the cycle ended with Clint. Everyone did not have the same number of gifts, but the procedure still worked out very well. No one except Sammy was overly surprised with the gifts they had received, as everyone had given enough hints so that they received what they had wanted or needed. Many hugs and handshakes were given during the opening ceremony.

Christmas dinner was memorable and was also very delicious.

Everyone had provided something for the meal and the desserts for later in the day. They all took some time to sing Christmas carols, and before having dessert, they went out into the snow and made a snowman, with which Sammy had a great time. They tried putting some vegetables on the snowman for a nose, eyes, a mouth, and even buttons, but Sammy kept taking them off the snowman and eating them. They then returned to the house for desserts and more coffee and talked for quite a long time again, and then Matt took Sammy and went home for the night.

The new year of 1858 arrived quite uneventfully. The families gathered together for the evening to enjoy one another's company and to ring in the new year at midnight. By midnight, Sammy was already asleep, but the rest welcomed midnight, sang "Auld Lang Syne," and then said a toast to the new year along with sharing prayers for a good year ahead. Clint and Ruby hugged each other and shared a long kiss. Matt and Becky looked at each other at that same time and stepped together for a hug and a short kiss, which seemed quite pleasant to them both. Harvey then shook hands with everyone and said, "None of that mush for me!"

Late in January, Matt went down to the dock area and visited the shipping company. He asked a couple of the men who regularly captained the shipping boats to please listen for anyone mentioning that they had horses to sell and when they were planning to do so, and then to let him know the location of those available horses and when they might be for sale. He also asked them to tell those horse owners that they knew of someone who would be interested in buying horses. The "captains" were not really captains but were given that title on the shipping boats just to clarify who was in command. January had been rather cold, but it had not snowed a great deal. February arrived and the groundhog saw its shadow, but no one knew what that meant so they ignored it. The month went by, and March arrived. Spring was getting closer.

Horsing around in the Spring

*T*oward the end of the first full week of March, one of the boat captains, C. Worthy Leader, found Matt and told him that a settler from near Fort Calhoun wished to sell some horses later that month. Matt expressed his thanks for the message and asked if he could send a note with the captain to the horse owner on his next trip up that way. By good fortune, the next trip would be in just a day or two, as shipping was beginning to commence again on a regular and daily basis. The captain agreed and waited while Matt composed a note.

It took Matt about ten minutes to get his thoughts down the way he wanted, and he put the note into an envelope with the horse owner's name on the outside. In the note, he had asked the owner how much he wanted for each horse, what kind of horses were they, their ages, whether they were mares or stallions, and how soon he might be able to come up there and take a look at them. He gave the message to the captain, who told him that the letter would be delivered to the horse owner on Monday because the boat didn't go out on Sundays. Matt said, "You're not horsing around, are you?" C. Worthy just snickered.

On Tuesday afternoon, C. Worthy returned to the dock from his trip up the Missouri and made his way to Matt's office with a response from the horse dealer. Matt was there doing paperwork, and he quickly opened the response and read it. He asked the captain if he could write a return note that night and get it to him by morning for delivery, and the captain said, "Sure thing." Matt asked what time the boat would be leaving in the morning and told the captain that he'd be there in plenty of time.

Matt then spent some time going over the information that had been sent. The seller wanted seventy-five dollars for the stallion and fifteen dollars each for his mares and geldings. He said that they were mainly work horses but could be used for other purposes, too. The man said Matt could come anytime and look over what was available. Matt decided to ride the boat up to Fort Calhoun the next day to meet the seller and see the horses in person. He would take his own horse onto the boat, if possible, and once he got to Fort Calhoun, he would have two options: either ride back to Bellevue leading his new horses or stay the night and ride back on the boat on Thursday.

He then went to the Forster house to see if they would be able to watch Sammy overnight on Wednesday. They said that would be no problem. Matt got his other arrangements made that night, took Sammy over to the Forster house the next morning, and then rode down to the shipping dock to ask the captain if he could ride the boat and bring his horse along on the trip. Both were okay with Captain C. Worthy.

The shipping boat made its first stop in Omaha, arriving there at about ten thirty. They left Omaha about fifteen minutes later and arrived at Fort Calhoun just after eleven o'clock. Matt led his horse off the boat, with several ropes laid over the horse in front of the saddle so he could lead any new horses onto the boat or home to Bellevue over land. He asked the captain what time he would return to the dock the next day and was told that they were usually back at approximately two o'clock to two thirty on their downriver trip. Matt promised that he'd be there in plenty of time if he intended to ride the boat back to Bellevue. Then, just to be certain, he asked the captain how many horses he could bring aboard if he thought it necessary to take them back to Bellevue that way. The captain said that six or eight horses would be no problem.

After ascertaining from the captain exactly where the horse seller's ranch was located, Matt disembarked from the boat with his horse. He arrived at the man's ranch before noon. The seller, Stan Hardy, took him to the corral where the horses for sale were located. The stallion, of course, was not in the same corral or there would have been more commotion going on. Matt asked Stan about the horses that were available and was told that Stan had purchased several horses early the previous winter and had kept them until now, but he had found that he didn't need them all. He also couldn't afford the additional hay and grain the horses consumed. He said that they were all good horses, gave their approximate ages, told Matt of any problems he'd had with any of them, told him which were geldings and which would probably be good broodmares, and also answered any other questions that Matt had. Next, they went to look at the stallion that was available. The seller had two other stallions and did not need to keep a third one. Matt asked him if this stallion was reliable in doing his duties, and the seller said that he was; in fact, he might be a little too enthusiastic.

They talked more, and Matt decided to purchase the available stallion, four good broodmares, and three other horses that would make good riding horses or would be strong enough to help with grain planting and harvest. They discussed the prices again, and Matt offered the man a hundred and seventy-five dollars—the seventy-five he'd asked for the stallion plus a total of one hundred dollars for the other seven horses. They agreed to the sale, then Matt asked him about the Fort Calhoun area and what was unique about its history.

Stan told him that Fort Calhoun had been platted only three years earlier, in 1855. It was named after John C. Calhoun, the secretary of war for the United States around 1820. Back in 1819,

President James Monroe had sent a military expedition called the Yellowstone Expedition to establish a series of forts along the Missouri River. They stopped to build Cantonment Missouri as a winter camp along the river bottom, below the bluffs, before trying to head on upstream in the spring. The winter proved to be harsh on them due to a combination of bitterly cold weather and a scurvy outbreak that befell the men due to lack of sufficient vitamin C and other essentials. More than two hundred men died during the winter.

In the spring of 1820, the Missouri River flooded near Cantonment, and they were forced to build a permanent camp (fort) atop what was then called Council Bluff (not the same location as present-day Council Bluffs, Iowa). The group named this new location Fort Atkinson after the commander of their expedition, but there had been discussion at that time about naming it Fort Calhoun. The expedition did not do much more exploring to the north and instead began conducting meteorological observations as research for the government.

The garrison was involved in combat only in 1823, against the Arikara tribes in southern South Dakota. The Arikara had attacked a trading party, and the troops from Fort Atkinson were sent to address the issue. Not one soldier was killed in the skirmish, but ironically, seven men died when one of their keelboats struck a log on the river. Those seven were counted as the first seven soldiers to die during the Indian Wars on the Great Plains. In 1827, the army abandoned the fort there and reassigned its personnel to other locations.

The fort then began declining into obscurity until 1846, when the Mormons established Cutler's Park in North Omaha and found some old provisions in the remnants of the fort. By the early 1850s, little remained of the fort and people still around the area became residents of Fort Calhoun instead. However, it is an interesting fact that Fort Atkinson was considered by historians to be the first town settlement in the Nebraska Territory, preceding Bellevue by many years.

Matt thanked Stan for his historical narrative of the area, then asked him if there was a place for him to stay overnight in the town. It was now late in the afternoon, and he had decided to wait until the next day to take the boat back to Bellevue. Stan invited Matt to stay overnight at his home, and Matt gratefully accepted the offer. They had a nice supper, and Matt talked with Stan and his wife until after nine o'clock, when they went to bed.

The next day, Matt woke from dreams of horses, and Mrs. Hardy gave him breakfast. When it was time, Matt rounded up his horses, put ropes on all of them, and led them into town, trailing behind his own horse. Stan had agreed to follow him into town and lead the stallion behind Matt and the other horses so the stallion would not cause problems with the other horses. At the dock, they carefully kept the stallion away from the other horses and waited for the shipping boat to arrive.

Just after two o'clock, the ship pulled in to dock. Matt saw Captain C. Worthy Leader and let him know he had nine horses, including his own. He also stated that the stallion must be kept apart from the others. C. Worthy said that he had just the place for the stallion to be loaded. They sailed away from Fort Calhoun, stopped in Omaha, and arrived back at Bellevue just before four o'clock. Matt unloaded his horses, keeping the stallion at a distance.

He arranged to buy C. Worthy a couple of drinks at the trading post the next time his boat came into port. He then tied up his other seven new horses and took the stallion to his cabin, where he tied his rope to a tree and gave him some feed. Then he went back for the other seven horses and led them through town and out to his new property in the country. He put them all into the big fenced-in area, which had part of the watering trough at one side, and then went to the building to get some feed he had left there for this occasion. He took the feed out and scattered it into a feeding trough. With contentment, he watched as the horses began to get some nourishment after experiencing such an unusual break in their daily routine. Matt finished up all his work at the property around seven o'clock and headed back to town.

28

Near Tragedy

Unbeknownst to Matt or Clint, the fur trapper named Les Manners had returned to town the day before, on Wednesday. He had camped outside of town down near the trading post when he arrived late in the afternoon, and at midmorning the next day he had gone to the trading post to sell some furs or exchange them for other goods that he needed. He had experienced decent success in his fur trapping since the previous July and had survived the winter hunkered down in a cave about twenty miles away. His appearance had changed a great deal since July, as he now had a long beard and mustache and unruly hair due to not grooming for the past eight months. The previous July, he had been clean shaven and a lot more spruced up, as he had been back in town for several days at that time to trade goods and attend the festivities.

Les went into the trading post with his furs and laid them out for Barry Hyde to assess. Many of the pelts were in pristine shape, but others were rather shaggy and tattered. After about an hour, Barry had looked over all the furs and had arrived at an amount that he would pay Les for the entire lot. While Barry had been assessing the furs, Les had been looking over all the merchandise to see what items he would be interested in swapping or buying outright. He was unable to locate a couple of items that he wanted, so he asked Barry if he had them. Barry said that he did not carry those items because they were being sold only by the local hardware store. Les then showed Barry the items he would be interested in buying and asked how much each of them cost, and he also asked Barry how much he was willing to pay for the furs. Barry gave him the fur price and, in addition, told Les what the cost would be for the items Les was interested in.

They struck a deal, and Les walked out with a nice supply of cash, plus the other items he had bought. Les told Barry he'd see him again around the Fourth of July or later in the summer, and then he left with his new possessions, went back to where he had camped, and put the new items away in his cart. He then started a fire and cooked some food for a late lunch, which he ate while stretched out on a little rise that looked out over the river. He thought that his camping spot was a very peaceful place and one where he hoped to eventually settle down with a woman to be his companion.

About four o'clock, he decided it was time to head to the hardware store to get the items Barry had told him would be available there. He arrived at about a quarter after four and went in to look around. Brad approached and asked him if he could help him to find something. Les told Brad what he was interested in, and Brad took him to where they were located.

As they were walking, Les noticed Becky across the room, and he remembered her from the previous Fourth of July. As he was looking at the items he wanted to purchase, he started asking Brad a few questions, such as how business was going, if that lady across the store was a customer in need of Brad's help, whether the store accepted credit, and what time the store opened and closed so that he could plan for what he needed to buy that day and the next day. Brad unsuspectingly answered all his questions. He said that business was usually quite good; it had its highs and lows. He said the lady across the store was not a customer but an employee. He explained that the store normally did not issue credit unless the buyer was a long-standing customer and reliable town resident and that the store normally closed at 6:00 but stayed open until 8:30 on Thursdays (which, of course, was that day). He also unwittingly informed the customer that he did not stay there on Thursday evenings after five thirty or six and that the lady across the store closed up for him on Thursday nights. The answers to the second and fourth questions almost made Les catch his breath.

He continued talking with Brad while surreptitiously stealing glances across the room at Becky. Finally, he decided on his purchases, paid Brad for them, and headed for the door. He had to walk by Becky on his way out, and she greeted him, "Hello, sir. Have a nice evening." He responded in kind: "Thanks, lady. I'll sure try." He looked right at her when he said that, and she looked back at him without a flicker of recognition in her face or her eyes. He went out the door and rode back to his camp, first stopping at the trading post to buy some liquor. He then rode to his camp and deposited his purchases. He was planning to depart the next day but began trying to decide on one more thing he might buy that evening. He finished off several drinks to get his courage up, and his lust for Becky began to intensify.

Les knew that Becky would be at the hardware store until eight o'clock or later. He made his plan to try to intercept her after she finished her work shift. He planned to accost her and perhaps rape her, depending on her reaction to his advances. In case she decided to close early, he thought he would get there at seven o'clock or shortly thereafter and keep an eye on the store. He rode his horse up to the main street and then down it, looking for a good place to wait inconspicuously where he would still be able to see the door to the store. About fifty yards down the street from the store, he noticed a couple of trees with a growth of bushes between them.

He figured that the area by the trees would be close enough to the store to intercept her, regardless of which way she went when she left. He rode on past those bushes to the next corner and went down the little side street there. At the end of the side street, he found a place to tie up his horse, which he left there for a quick and easy escape. Then he slowly made his way across the area between his horse and the bushes over by Main Street. It was now about twenty minutes after seven o'clock, and he was in position.

Over in the hardware store, Becky was keeping busy restocking some of the shelves and also sweeping up the area in preparation for closing. It had not been a busy evening so far, and Brad had told her previously that if things were quiet, she was welcome to close up the store a little early. She had left early on a few occasions previously but never before 7:45. That time came and no one else had come to the store or even walked by the front of the building, so she decided to lock up and head home. She put out the lanterns in the store, went outside, locked the door, and started down the street right in the direction of those bushes across the street.

Shortly after seven o'clock, Matt had begun his ride into town from his property out in the country, where he had just put his new horses for the evening. He rode at a leisurely pace from the property and into the town, heading for the Forster house to pick up Sammy. He got to their house at about seven thirty, and Ruby answered the door. She informed him that Sammy was already asleep, as they hadn't known if Matt would make it back that night. Ruby then asked if Matt would like to stay for a while because Becky would be home from work soon. Matt had forgotten that Becky worked that evening at the store and felt kind of guilty about forgetting. He told Ruby that he was just going to walk on down to the store to meet Becky and walk back home with her. Ruby told him that it was a great idea.

Becky walked down the street about fifty yards from the store when, all of a sudden, a man stepped out from behind the bushes and blocked her path. He smelled of liquor and said he had been waiting to talk to her. She was startled and taken aback by his sudden appearance, and she asked him who he was and why he wanted to talk. He said it was because she was so pretty, and he wanted to get to know her better. His arrogance and boldness made her angry, and she asked him why he thought she would be interested in him or even attracted to him. He said that he could tell that she wanted him. At this comment, she laughed and said that he must be daft to think that she would be interested in him. Her confidence and honesty angered him, and he rushed at her, grabbed her wrist firmly, and pulled her back behind the bushes. There he started groping at her and trying to kiss her. He tried to pull some of her clothes off, and she screamed. Furious, he hit her hard and knocked her down, stunning her.

Matt had started toward the main street just after 7:45. It wasn't a long walk to the hardware store, and he figured he'd easily be there before 8:00, when it normally closed. He was about halfway there when he heard angry voices arguing and then a scream. He ran in that direction, and as he came upon the bushes, he heard muffled noises from behind them, as if there was something going on back there. He raced around the bushes and saw a man on the ground wrestling with someone who was under him.

Matt said, "What are you doing? What's going on?" The man jumped up and turned toward him, but Matt could barely see him in the dim light. Matt thought it looked like he was reaching for his belt. He could not see who was on the ground, but he thought maybe it was Becky. Then Becky cried, "Matt, help! This man—he's attacking me!" Matt wanted to pound the man into submission, but he thought first of making sure that Becky was okay. He then told the man to immediately leave or he would be sorry. The man kind of snarled and started lunging toward Matt. Matt instinctively dodged to the left and kicked at the legs of the drunken man as he lumbered by. The man crashed to the ground and groaned. Matt turned and immediately pinned him down the prone man, who was lying at an odd angle with one shoulder raised up a bit. Matt soon realized that the man was not struggling at all. He stopped restraining him, shook him, and then got up, pulling Becky to him as she rushed into his arms. He kissed her and asked her if she was all right. They continued embracing each other tightly. Matt had a sudden revelation of how incredibly important this young woman had become to him.

Matt then quickly checked the man again, but he still was not moving. Since there was no light to see what had actually happened to him, Matt decided to just leave him there for now and take Becky to her house.

They walked back to the Forster house and quickly told Clint and Ruby what had happened. Ruby took Becky under her wing and went into the other room to examine her. Clint and Matt got a lantern and walked back to the area of the bushes, with Clint leading his horse behind them. They went behind the bushes and found the man still sprawled there on the ground. They turned him over and found that a big hunting knife was sticking out of his chest. The man had apparently pulled his knife on Matt in the dim light and then rushed him. Matt had been extremely fortunate to evade the knife attack, and to save Becky, too.

They did not recognize the man because of his shaggy beard, and they discussed what to do with him. They decided they couldn't just leave him there overnight, so they lifted him over the back of Clint's horse and carried his body over to Matt's cabin. They put it in a protected area until the next day, when they would turn him over to the mayor. Matt then had Clint take a look at the new stallion, since he was there. Clint rode his horse home while Matt gave his new stallion some feed, talking quietly to him and stroking his head and neck for a while. Then Matt went inside. He anguished over what had occurred and that a man was dead, even though Matt himself had not intended for that to happen. Still, it was a fact that weighed on his mind. Finally, Matt's fatigue from a long day and from the arduous altercation overcame him, and he drifted off to sleep.

29

A Day of Work, Reflection, and Progress

The next morning, Matt ate some breakfast early, got dressed, and then went outside to feed the stallion again. Just after seven thirty, Clint rode up, leading another horse behind him. He had found it tied to a tree on his way over and suspected it might belong to the man who they were now going to take down to the smithy to turn over to the mayor. They draped the man over the saddle of the newly discovered horse for the ride down to Main Street.

They got down to the smithy, and Henry was already busy. He looked the body over while listening to Matt's story from the night before. He asked them if they knew who the man was. Clint said that he wasn't certain who it was but that there seemed to be something familiar about him, now that he could see him in the light of day. Henry asked Clint if he would take over at the smithy for a while so that he could take the man around the town to see if anyone knew who he was. Clint said that he would cover things at the forge, and Matt headed back to his cabin to get the stallion and take him out to his rural property. He didn't have to worry about

Sammy that morning because he had stayed overnight at the Forster house.

After getting his horses settled down for the day, Matt rode around to several of the homes of the new settlers and asked them if they would help him build a house on his property during the next few weeks. Because of his prior assistance to them, they all agreed to be part of a house-raising party, whenever he could get it organized. He went back to his office and drew up diagrams for the new house, then went to the hardware store to order all the materials for building it.

Meanwhile, Henry had first gone to the newspaper office with the horse and corpse and found Daniel there. He asked Daniel if he recognized the man, but he did not. He told Daniel what had occurred the previous night, and they agreed that the man's death had been a result of self-defense. They deemed the death an accident and decided they would find a burial place for the man somewhere in or around town that day. Henry then took the man to the hardware store and told Brad and Penny the story, and they were both upset and saddened that it had been a horrible experience for Becky. They went outside to view the man's body, and Brad was aghast when he realized it was the man who had come into the store the previous afternoon. He thought the man had said his name was Les, he said, and he had bought some things and additionally had asked some questions and talked with Brad for a while. As Brad related the questions that the man had asked him, they both realized that his questions about the other "lady customer" and the information Brad had given about the store staying open until later that night, with Becky there alone, were major factors in what had resulted.

Henry thanked them and then stopped briefly at the bank and the post office, but no one there knew the man or had seen him before. Last, he rode to the trading post, where Barry informed him that the man's name was Les Manners and that he was a fur trader who only came into Bellevue about twice a year. He also was the man who had been at the Fourth of July party last summer and had a row with Clint, in regard to Becky. They talked a bit more, and Barry told him that he thought the man had been camping just to the north of the trading post, close to the river. When Henry heard who the man was, he wondered for an instant if perhaps Matt had actually known who it was and had taken revenge by stabbing the man himself. Regardless, he thought, Matt still would have been justified, as he was protecting Becky.

Henry then rode up the river bank a short distance and discovered a place with the remnants of a small campfire, where a tent was set up and a small cart was sitting. He looked inside the cart and under some blankets, where he found the items that had been bought the previous day at both the trading post and the hardware store. He took the body of Les off his horse and laid it near the edge of the small rise nearby, then got a blanket and covered his body with it. He tied the man's horse to the cart and rode back to town to get a couple of shovels and to ask Daniel, who was a town alderman, to help bury the man. They rode back down to the riverbank and dug a grave and buried Les near the river on which the man had done lots of trapping in recent years. They then hitched the man's horse up to the cart and took both to the smithy, where they would put the horse, the cart, and the supplies up for sale, with the proceeds going to the town treasury.

Matt, meanwhile, had first gone over to the Forster place to check on Becky and to see Sammy. After assuring himself that things were okay there, he went back to his cabin and led his new stallion out to the rural property. He guided the stallion into the inner corral that he had constructed, which also had a water trough and a feed trough, just like the bigger fenced-in area. The stallion immediately went over to the outside fence of his corral, where he could be nearest to the other horses, and began whinnying at them. Matt thought that the whinny sounded like he was saying, *Come on over here, you sweet ladies.* But Matt ignored him, as did the other horses, and Matt went about getting feed from the main structure and feeding the horses in the main corral and then pumping some more water for them. After that he took some feed into the stallion's smaller corral and checked to make certain he had water, too. He looked inside the building structure to mentally inventory what supplies were still remaining in the storage area and what he might need to purchase in order to replenish those supplies. He then departed from the rural property and headed south on his horse, with a plan in mind for the rest of the day.

Matt rode south at a more than leisurely pace for an hour until he reached the northern banks of the Platte River, right where it converged into the Missouri. He got off his horse and tied it to a tree, then began walking back and forth along the bank of the Platte, stopping occasionally to stare down the west bank of the mighty Missouri River. His thoughts turned back to that fateful day early the previous June, when the Platte and the Missouri had conspired to take his wife's life.

Matt knew that he was there to say his final goodbyes to Amy and to move on with his life. He finally stopped in a place that had a very good view of the Missouri and its west bank. He bowed his head, as he had done a hundred times since last June, and prayed for Amy's soul, prayed for his son, and prayed for the Forster family. He thanked God for giving him the fortitude to get through this ordeal and for guiding him in his new life in Bellevue. He knew that there had been a strong intervention from somewhere, a divine force that was helping him make the decisions that he had made after reaching Bellevue. He then raised his head toward the sky and said, "Amy, you know that I loved you dearly and that I have missed you intensely. You provided me with a wonderful marriage and with a wonderful son. But I know now that I need to move on with my life. I know how much Becky meant to you, and I also how much she has meant to Sammy. It is my intent to begin courting Becky and to eventually marry her. It is time for me to take that step, and I know that you are up there above giving me your full approval. I will never forget you and all the many things that we did together and accomplished. May you have a peaceful and joyous eternity with our Father, who is in heaven with you. Amen!"

Matt then mounted his horse again after having spent more than an hour at the site of the tragedy, and he headed back to Bellevue, feeling an aura of good vibrations coming to him from Amy and further fortifying his plans for when he got back to Bellevue that day. He arrived at about three o'clock and went immediately to the Forster house. Becky was sitting in the kitchen area with Sammy and Ruby, cutting some vegetables and meat for their supper that night. Matt sat down and asked Becky how she was feeling now, and she said that she was fine, again thanking him for his intervention the night before.

He then told them what Clint and he had done that morning and related that things were looking good out at his rural property. He did not mention his ride down to the Platte. Ruby invited him to have supper with them, and he accepted. Then he said that he should go back out to his rural property to give the horses some feed again and get them taken care of for the night. Sammy wanted to go with him so that he could see the horses, so Matt loaded Sammy onto the horse in front of him and between his arms and they rode out to the property together. They took care of the feeding and upkeep that was necessary. Sammy even got to pet the head of one of the tame broodmares, and he cackled with delight as he did so. Matt finished up everything at the property, and they rode back to the Forster house for supper.

Clint was home by the time Matt got back, and he told the group what Henry had told him about the man who had died the night before. He was surprised, as were all the others, that it was the same man who had accosted Becky the previous Fourth of July. Clint had seen the man up close and personal the previous year, and he had felt a glint of recognition but had been unable to place the man until Henry told him who he was. They then had their supper and continued their conversation about that man and also about some upcoming things they needed to do. After supper was completed, Matt asked Becky if she would go on a walk with him, and she agreed to do so. They left the Forster house and walked rather slowly, but comfortably, to the high bank overlooking the river.

Once they were in the location Matt wanted, where they had enjoyed the picnic last summer, Matt told Becky that he had some things he'd like to say to her. He took her hands, looked into her eyes, and said, "Becky, I must tell you what has been going on in my mind and where I am right now. Last June, I was devastated by the loss of Amy, and I decided to stay here in Bellevue with Sammy. Then you and your family made the same decision. Through all these changes, you've given me loyal support and have provided dedicated care for Sammy. You mean the world to him, and you have also become very important to me. Last night was a real scare for me, and it put things in perspective. I knew how much you meant to me, but the incident really thrust that realization to the forefront. I rode down to the Platte River today and stood across from where Amy was swept away, and I prayed and said my goodbyes to her. I told her that I intend to begin courting you, if you accept me, and that I knew she would approve because of the very close relationship that the two of you had. As I started to ride back to Bellevue, I had this aura of peace settle over me, and I knew that she had given the idea her blessing. In actuality, you and I have already gone through a great deal of what would normally be a courting process. I now realize for certain that I love you, and I hope that you feel the same way too. I want to ask you right now if we can officially begin an engagement process and formulate a plan to get married."

Becky looked up at him and said, "I'll give it some thought." Matt stood there, suddenly a little uncomfortable, and then she said, "Of course I'll marry you! I've been waiting and waiting for you to be ready." She threw her arms around his neck and kissed him passionately. After the kiss, he stepped back, looked down at her, and said, "Is that the best you've got?" She laughed and then gave it another try, which turned out to be as good as or better than the first try. They then stood next to each other and enjoyed the moment, while gazing out at the mighty river that had now brought them together for the rest of their lives. Matt said, "Let's go back to your house and announce our engagement." Becky agreed.

They walked back into the Forster house, holding hands as they came in the door. All the rest of the Forster family and Sammy were sitting in the main room talking and relaxing. Matt let go of Becky's hand, walked over toward Clint, and said, "Clint, I want you to be my father-in-law. Is that okay with you, Dad?" Clint got an astonished look on his face, and then he grinned from ear to ear. He arose from his chair and said, "Well, if I have to be your father-in-law, I guess I can live with it." Ruby put her hands over her mouth and began crying, then arose and gave both Becky and Matt long hugs. Sammy looked at everyone and asked what was going on. Matt knelt next to Sammy and told him that Becky was going to be his new mother and would soon be living with them. Sammy then ran and jumped into Becky's arms and hugged her. Harvey had remained in the background, and he said "Whatever!" But he also smiled to himself. He was one of Matt's biggest fans.

The group then sat around for the next hour and discussed things. Ruby wanted to know if they had any idea when the wedding would be. Becky said that they hadn't discussed any exact dates yet, but if Matt still wanted to marry her a month or so later, she would be ready for it. Matt said to her, "So soon?" They all chuckled. They would have to set a date, talk to Preacher Devine, figure out who all to invite, decide on a wedding party, and discuss having a reception.

Clint had found some libations in the pantry, and they all toasted one another as they talked. They had a great time, staying up later than usual, and then Matt took Sammy home to their cabin. The next day would be the start of the weekend, but lots of things still needed to be done. It had been a very full, rewarding, and emotional day, and Matt was definitely ready for sleep. However, getting to sleep still proved difficult due to all the excitement that had built up in him.

30

The Rest of Spring and the Wedding

Things continued to evolve as spring went by. Clint kept busy with his blacksmith trade, and Ruby started teaching again in April. Harvey decided not to attend school any longer, and he instead spent his time out on the properties fixing things and building new things. Becky continued watching Sammy and also working a couple of days at the hardware store, but after her horrible incident, she requested a change in her hours on Thursday so she wouldn't have to close the store alone anymore.

Matt also spent a lot of time at the rural property. He established a workable rotation for the broodmares to take turns visiting the stallion, observing their behaviors daily. He tried to keep watch a little to see if anything had occurred that might lead to a foal in the spring. He also had drawn up plans for a new house, ordered the materials. and set up two Saturdays for late April and early May when several of the settlers would come over to help him build a house on his property. Harvey also came out to help, and Clint joined in after he finished work at the smithy.

The workers also helped Matt with the expansion of his storage structure into a barn of sorts and later helped build another storage shed and a couple of lean-to structures for the horses, to protect them better from the elements. He continued surveying and platting other properties out in the rural area, recording them in his notebooks that had now turned into ledgers. He took Sammy to work with him in the office every day that Becky worked at the hardware store, and they always had lunch together and discussed their plans for the future. Soon after their engagement, Matt also ordered a new bed and dresser, two new easy chairs, and a new dining room table with four chairs. He hoped they would arrive by the wedding day, but if not, he and Becky would make do with what he had on hand at present.

They were now looking at a wedding date of May 29, a Saturday, when more people would be available to attend because they would be free of work constraints. They had spoken to Preacher Devine about two possible dates a couple of weeks earlier, and true to his word, he got back to them within a couple of days. He told them their preferred date of May 29, at 4:00 p.m., would work fine.

Matt had considered writing a letter to his parents asking if they could attend the wedding, but the date was fast coming up on them and he decided that he didn't want to delay or compromise their plans. He figured that he would notify them of the marriage date and let them decide if they could come or not. After all, they hadn't attended his first wedding. Regardless, he mailed them a letter with the wedding announcement, figuring that it was a futile effort.

Not having made many close friends in town up until now, both Matt and Becky had difficulty in deciding who they would have stand up with them at the wedding. Of course, Clint would give Becky away and Sammy would be the ring bearer, but they must find a maid of honor and a best man. Becky had made some acquaintances of young women who were customers of the hardware store and whom she had also seen in church. Matt had also made some acquaintances at the church, plus C. Worthy Leader through their meetings for drinks at the trading post and his friendships with some of the new settlers.

They finally made their decisions after talking to a couple of the people under consideration. Becky settled on a young lady named Priscilla Byers, whom she talked to regularly at both the store and the church, for her maid of honor. Additionally, she chose two others from church, Bonnie Lassey and Mae Flowers, as her bridesmaids. Matt chose C. Worthy Leader as his best man. He chose one new settler named Claude Buster, with whom he had gotten along quite well, and then Harvey, Becky's brother, as his two groomsmen. Preacher Devine would, of course, conduct the ceremony. Matt also arranged for a wedding reception down on the river, using one of the shipping company's largest boats. The trading post agreed to cater the event, with a fine array of libations and some really delicious barbecue, potato salad, baked beans, cakes, and pies. The shipping company would provide a couple of lifeguards in case someone fell off the boat. Everything now seemed ready for the event.

The rest of May went by with preparations continuing, including practicing the ceremony with Preacher Devine. Matt had continued with his clerking work and also had begun furnishing the new house, mainly with items from the hardware store but also some from the trading post. Becky helped him pick out several items, including kitchen supplies, a table and chairs, some living room furniture, and many other items. Matt and his friends got everything moved into the new house, and Becky approved the placement of the items. Soon thereafter, Matt received a letter from his parents saying they would not make it for the wedding, but they sent him a check for twenty-five hundred dollars, which stunned him.

May 29 arrived, and everyone spent the day preparing for the 4:00 p.m. ceremony. Becky got to the church early in the afternoon, and her mother helped her get dressed and ready. The maid of honor arrived about an hour later and the other two bridesmaids shortly thereafter. Matt got to the church fairly early as well, already in his best suit (which was also his only suit). His best man and groomsmen arrived about an hour before the ceremony, and he again went over the details with them.

Around three thirty, guests began arriving, signing a registry book as they came in. Just before the ceremony, Matt and his entourage walked out to a place near the chancel. Right at 4:00, the preacher took his place, and the music began for the entrance of the rest of the wedding party. Sammy came in, carrying the ring on a small pillow he held out in front of him. Mae walked in next and met up with Claude at the front, and they went together up onto the chancel, splitting off to the left and right when they got to the proper location at the altar. Next, Bonnie met up with Harvey, and they went up to their places on the chancel. Priscilla and C. Worthy completed the wedding party, and they went up onto the chancel and took their places. After a short but dramatic pause, the music changed to the familiar chords of "Here Comes the Bride," and Clint and Becky marched up the aisle. They reached the front of the church, and Preacher Devine asked, "Who gives this woman to this man?" Clint responded, "Her mother and I do," and then he went to sit by Ruby. Becky took Matt's arm, and they ascended to the chancel. After the appropriate ceremony and the tradition of the ring ceremony, the preacher pronounced them man and wife. They kissed each other with ardor and enthusiasm, and then they led the wedding party outside. The bride, groom, and remainder of the wedding party formed a line and greeted guests as they came out, thanking them for their attendance. They also asked each guest to join them at the boat dock for the evening festivities.

Down at the boat dock, the newly married couple and the wedding party, joined by Becky's parents, began greeting guests around five o'clock. Guests went on board and were free to wander around the boat, look at the river, snack on whatever they could find, or locate the bar for refreshments or spirits. In actuality, many guests started out by drinking first and then looked around the boat. The party went well. Everyone feasted on the great food, and many toasts were made. The most notable toasts were from the best man,

C. Worthy Leader, and the one from Clint, who praised this union of his wonderful daughter with a man who had so much integrity and vitality and insight. Matt thought, *I couldn't have said it better myself.* The party came to an end at about dusk, and everyone went home. Sammy stayed the night at the Forster household to give the new bride and groom some privacy and time to unwind. No one is sure if anything else happened for the rest of that night. We do know, though, that the new bed had arrived at the hardware store several days earlier and was now in the new house.

The Bellevue Presbyterian Church with original
steeple (before the tornado of 1908).
(Photo courtesy Nebraska State Historical Society.)

The Ensuing Summer

y mid-June, Matt and Becky had everything moved from the log cabin to the new house out in the country, and they had settled into a regular routine. Each day, they got up early, had breakfast, took care of horses, worked through the rest of the day, had supper, went to bed, and often got frisky—day after day after day! On Tuesday and Thursday, all three of the little family rode into town together and worked all day. Becky worked at the hardware store and Matt next door at the city clerk's office. Sammy went back and forth between the two stores, depending on where he could get the better deal. All the other days, they pretty much remained out in the country, doing tasks on their property. Matt sometimes went around to check on neighbors or to survey and plat additional property. One night a week, the rest of the Forster family would come out to their horse ranch and have supper. On either Tuesday or Thursday, they would go to the Forster house for supper after getting off work.

On Sundays they met the Forster family at church, then shared a meal either at the Forster house or at the trading post. Both Matt and Becky began noticing that Harvey seemed to be spending more and more time talking with Bonnie Lassey at church, with whom he had been paired up at the wedding. They both thought that it was quite unusual for Harvey to be doing so much talking. The cat must have given his tongue back to him.

About that time, Matt received another letter from his parents saying that they were planning to come visit in early August. They would try to write again when they were leaving Kentucky to let Matt know approximately when they would arrive in Bellevue. Matt sent a letter back to them expressing his happiness that they would be coming to visit. He promised them a good time.

July Fourth came around again, and they all essentially repeated the events of the year before, except for the final encounter they'd had with the drunken vagabond at the cookout by the trading post. Also, this year, they were accompanied by Bonnie. They had a nice meal on Main Street again, followed by a boat ride on the river and the barbecue at the trading post. Throughout the entire day, they constantly talked with new friends they'd met and an assortment of people they'd rather not see anymore. Matt was becoming a very well-known and respected citizen of the town, and Becky was also starting to gain many admirers and friends. Speaking of admirers, Harvey was kind of googly eyed-around Bonnie. All in all, everyone had a great day in celebrating the Fourth of July.

July roared by seemingly quickly, what with all the usual daily tasks and activities, plus planning that needed to be made for the visitation of Matt's parents. About mid-July, Matt had found a settler who did not want to farm to buy the old log cabin. He was very pleased to get rid of that second home and also to provide a good location for a new settler. Clint and Harvey also were starting to make improvements on their rural properties, and both were beginning the construction of main houses. Harvey had planted corn, wheat, and oats on both properties in the spring, and he would be harvesting his crops in a couple of months.

By the end of July, Matt and Becky were ready for Matt's parents to visit. They had set up the old beds that Matt had used in the log cabin and made a space for Sammy to sleep out in the main living area so that Matt's parents could have Sammy's room. They had brought home some extra supplies of vegetables, fruit, and cooking oil, too. Matt's parents' last letter indicated that they would arrive during the first week of August, and they planned to cross the Missouri River on the ferry from the Iowa side over to Bellevue.

Matt conversed several times with Will Ford in regard to this crossing, and he was assured that a runner would be sent from the dock to Matt's house the moment the boat carrying his parents got to the dock. He was kind of excited about their visit but also apprehensive. He had not seen them for about five years now, since about eighteen months or so before Sammy's birth. He had been trying to prepare Sammy for their visit and explain who they were and some of the reasons that Sammy had never met them before.

His parents arrived, and a rider was sent to Matt's house with the news, as promised. He immediately hitched up two horses to the wagon and headed for town. He went straight to the dock and gave them great big hugs. They greeted one another and talked for a bit, and then he loaded up their luggage onto the wagon, got them aboard, and headed back to the house, where Becky was preparing a good meal for the evening. When they arrived at the house, Becky carried Sammy out to greet Matt's parents, Benjamin and Susan. Sammy was a little shy at first, then his grandma gave him a big hug and his grandpa gave him some rock candy and another big hug. Matt introduced Becky, and she immediately welcomed and embraced both of Matt's parents. Matt took the luggage, led them into the house, and showed them around, including where they would be sleeping and where everything else was located, including the frontier plumbing (often called an outhouse). They chatted for a bit, and then Matt said, "Sammy, let's go show them our horses." Sammy grinned and said, "Yes, let's do it." They walked out and looked into the corrals, and many of the horses came over, expecting a treat. The horses were not disappointed, as Matt had planned for the occasion with a bucket of feed and some carrots. They fed and touched the horses for a while, then Matt showed them the other buildings and corrals on his property. Gesturing across the spread of his property, Matt briefly outlined how all this land had come into his possession and how much of his success was a result of information received from J. Sterling Morton, along with his own investigations into obtaining property and recording it. He told them about his office in town as well as many other things. Then, they went back into the house, where Becky had supper ready and the table all set.

Since his parents arrived on a Friday, they all spent Saturday touring the main street and the rest of the town, went by the log cabin where he and Sammy had lived for the first year, and then stopped at the Forster house so that Matt's parents could meet the rest of Becky's family. They stayed there for a while, exchanging pleasantries and making plans to attend church the next day, to be followed by sharing a big meal at the Forster house.

They then left the Forster house and went down by the river, and Matt showed them all the companies that were down there. On the way back home, he drove them by many of the new properties out in the countryside and showed them the two locations owned by Becky's parents and her brother. They spent the rest of the day and evening back at their country house, attempting to catch up on as much information as they could from the past five years. Matt's mom and dad also paid a great deal of attention to Sammy, and he quickly became enamored of them as well. They all went to bed at a fairly early hour, as they had several plans for the next day.

The church service the next day was nice. Preacher Devine and many of the other congregants were introduced to Matt's parents, and many kind words were exchanged back and forth. They then rode back to the Forster house for their big dinner. They stayed there all afternoon, talking and exchanging stories, and it got so late in the afternoon that they stayed there for supper, too. Afterward, they rode back out to the country house and eventually settled down for the night.

Matt's father had brought with him a new camera that he had

purchased a year or so earlier in Kentucky, and he always was busy staging and taking pictures. His camera was a daguerreotype. A French man, Louis Jacques Monde Daguerre, had begun developing photography in the early 1830s. He was able to attain high contrast and extremely sharp images by exposing his image on a plate coated with silver iodine and then exposing this plate again to mercury vapor. By 1837, he was able to fix the images with a common salt solution. He called this process daguerreotyping and tried unsuccessfully for a couple of years to commercialize his system. In 1839, the first photographic camera was built by Alphonse Giroux, who signed a contract with Daguerre to produce the camera in France. The early daguerreotype camera required long exposure times, which in 1830 ranged from five to thirty minutes. In the United States, there were several daguerreotype cameras, with one known as the Lewis type coming to the forefront in 1851. The Lewis camera utilized a bellows for focusing, and it enabled the user to make a second, in-camera copy of the original image. This was the kind of camera purchased by Matt's father, Benjamin, in 1855.

The next day, Matt took Benjamin out to help with the morning chores, and the two of them spent a while riding to various locations and talking to some of the new settlers. His parents had made arrangements to go back across the river on the ferry, where they would meet other travelers heading to Kentucky, the following Monday, after spending nine days with Matt and his family. Matt's dad asked him if he would consider moving back to Kentucky and taking over the horse farm there. Matt looked at his father a bit quizzically but then delicately declined, saying that he had now established a new life here in Bellevue. However, the question did make Matt feel a little uneasy and even a little guilty.

On Tuesday and Thursday, they all went to town, and Becky and Matt went to work while Matt's parents took Sammy around town for a few stops, including to the smithy to see Clint and to meet Henry. They also went to the bank and the newspaper office to introduce themselves, eventually ending up at the hardware store, where they met Brad and Penny and spent some time with Becky. During those two days, Matt also showed them his notebooks and ledgers and how he kept track of things. By then, he also had a filing cabinet and some other essential office supplies.

The next weekend came and went, with lots of exploration and further discussion on Saturday, and then church, dinner, and socializing on Sunday again. On Sunday, Benjamin presented Matt with the daguerreotype camera and the accompanying equipment and showed him how to use it, going over instructions several times. He said he'd buy a new one back in Kentucky but wanted Matt to keep this one.

Early on Monday morning, they all loaded up into the wagon and headed for the river. At the ferry, there were lots of teary eyes and well wishes at their departure, and everyone waved almost the entire time the ferry was crossing the river. Matt had told his parents that he and Becky had discussed a possible trip to Kentucky to visit them the following summer. It depended, though, on whether things were settled down in Bellevue by then. If they couldn't arrange it for next summer, then they would try for the summer of 1860. Matt and his family then rode back to the country and went home.

Eight days later, around noon on a Tuesday, Matt was sitting in his office working on his books when the door opened, and in walked Billy Banks, their former wagon master. Billy had asked at the bank how to find Matt and had been given directions to his office. Matt was astonished and quite happy to see him walk in. They shook hands, gave each other a big hug, and slapped each other on the back. They started talking rapidly, asking questions and relating information, until Matt thought that maybe they should be sharing this discussion with Becky, especially since Billy would only be visiting for the remainder of the day. He had to get back on the trail to Louisville before wintry weather hit and prevented further travel.

Matt informed Billy that he and Becky were now married and that she was working at the hardware store next door. Billy smiled and said that he was not surprised that Matt and Becky had wed. They went over to her store, and the three of them had a nice, long discussion. Sammy, who happened to be in the hardware store with Becky, looked quizzically at Billy, like he knew him from somewhere. When they told Sammy that Billy was with the wagon train, Sammy came over and hugged both of Billy's knees. They continued exchanging information for an hour or so, and Becky asked if Billy would be able to have supper with them later that afternoon. He accepted but said that he could not stay too late.

Billy inquired about the rest of Becky's family, so they told Billy that Clint was working in the smithy just down at the end of the block and around the corner. Billy went over there to talk to Clint for a while. Billy told Clint that arrangements had already been made for all of them to have supper together but that he'd also be happy to treat them all at the trading post restaurant. Clint said that Ruby was fixing a big supper for them all and that Billy was more than welcome to come to their house and share in that meal, as there would be more than enough food prepared.

By then, Matt had locked up his office and gone over to the smithy. In a short while, he and Billy left and rode out into the country to see all their respective properties. They rode back into town about four o'clock, and Matt took Billy by his old log cabin, the mission school, and the Presbyterian church. Eventually, they went to the Forster house, where Ruby was busily cooking supper. She was delighted to see Billy and offered him a drink, but he said that he'd just have a glass of water. The meal went well, and the discussion was fast and furious, as they all recited their plans for the winter and for the next year. Billy planned to lead another wagon train west in late March or April, but he was becoming concerned about how long he'd be able to continue doing this kind of work, not only because of his age but also because of gossip and rumblings of conflict developing in the eastern United States over the slavery issue. Plus, Billy thought that he was getting close to retiring, and he actually had already applied for and paid the fee to secure a big plot of land in Oregon. He thought that maybe when he got there the next fall with his wagon train of 1859, he might just stay there for good. He wrote down the name of the town and the location of the property in case any of the others wanted to come to visit him in Oregon and go fish for some big salmon.

The wonderful evening of sharing stories came to an end, and Billy headed down to the ferry area, where he planned to sleep until the ferry crossed the river very early the next morning. Matt, Becky, and Sammy went home but continued discussing the many things Billy had told them. It was so nice to have seen him again, and they hoped he would have a successful wagon-train excursion the next year, followed by a wonderful life out west. Just before he had left, Matt told Billy that he planned to ride his horse to Kentucky to see his mother and sisters and asked Billy what the best route would be from Bellevue to Louisville. Billy said that he'd cross the river from Bellevue to Iowa, go straight across Iowa to Illinois, and then head down through Illinois and into Kentucky, near Louisville. He said that in this way he could avoid going through Missouri, which was having a lot of issues, discussion, and arguing going on in relation to slavery.

The rest of the summer and fall went by seemingly quickly but with all of them getting a lot of things done on their rural properties, including Harvey and Clint getting the crops harvested and their houses further developed. Harvey had done excellent work tending the crops that summer and fall, and his fields produced a great yield. Matt was getting more acreages platted, and they all continued to work in town during the week and go to church or socialize on occasion.

Thanksgiving was celebrated in a big way that year because they had a bumper crop that fall. The Christmas season went by with a great deal of joy and love. On Christmas Day, they all celebrated together after going to church that morning. The year 1858 was coming to an end, and they had now been in Bellevue for more than a year and a half.

New Life and More Progress in 1859

The new year of 1859 came in very cold and very snowy. They had so much snow in mid-January that all three households were cloistered in their homes for almost ten days. Finally, they were able to dig their way out and get to town for supplies.

Matt had moved the horses into the barn to feed them and keep them watered. The previous late April and early May, he had allowed the broodmares to go into the stallion's corral one at a time, and he was expecting to have some new foals in late spring. The gestation period for a horse is an average of 340 days, or 11 months. For horses and their owners, breeding success requires that the mares reach an estrous cycle, usually during nineteen to twenty-two days in the spring or early summer. The female becomes sexually responsive during those days, and her accepting behavior is noticeable and definitely sensed by the stallion. This cycle is in place so that foals will not be born during the harsh winter months, thereby decreasing their odds of survival. The mare is also called a dam, a baby horse is called a foal. A little older male is called a colt and a little older female is called a filly.

Based on the mating time, Matt expected to have foals arriving in late March to late April. He was anticipating them as he was anxious to increase the numbers in his herd and wanted to get his horse business growing faster. Soon, he would have several extra horses for sale or trade. Last fall, he had traded two of his other male horses for broodmares that someone else had previously owned, so in late spring of this year, he would have six healthy broodmares.

In January, Matt sent a letter to his parents saying that he, Becky, and Sammy would try to make it to Kentucky late in the summer, if things worked out all right. He mentioned again that his horses would be foaling sometime in the spring and that he would want to get them started out properly in life (on the right hoof, so to speak).

In early February, Becky dropped a bombshell when she informed Matt that she was pregnant, probably about four months along. Matt was overjoyed, as was Sammy when they told him. The next day after work, when they went to the Forster house for supper, they informed Becky's parents and Harvey of the news. Everyone was delighted. Clint said how wonderful it was. Ruby said that she was so happy for them and happy to be a new grandmother. Harvey said, "Whatever." In the next few days, they also informed their friends as well as all the business owners in town and down by the river. Matt realized that they would now not be able to go to Kentucky that summer after all, so he wrote his parents to let them know the situation.

Becky ordered a crib and some other necessities that they would need for the baby through the hardware store. Ruby made a baby blanket for them, and Harvey spent some spare time actually building a swing set for their yard. He was a little early with his project for the baby, but Sammy could use it in the meantime. Everyone was thinking of what they could do to help with taking care of the baby.

The new crib arrived in early April, along with a rocking chair and a baby's high chair that Becky had ordered. Brad Pincher showed them to Becky and told her that all three items were now gifts from him and his wife to Becky. Brad said to call it a kind of bonus for all her good work at the store. It is still not clear if Penny knew about this dealing or if she would have agreed with it. Maybe she was mellowing!

In early April, they got a letter from Matt's parents expressing their joy at the announcement of a new baby and saying they understood why Matt and Becky could not visit them during the coming summer. A couple of days later, one of the mares gave birth to the first foal at their new horse farm. It was a male foal, and it soon rose and moved around on long, wobbly legs, as foals are able to stand and even to run very early in their lives. Matt was happy, and he said, "Damn, she's good." About the middle of April, a second mare gave birth to a new foal, this time a female. Clint was there to witness this one, and he twirled his mustache and said, "Curses! Foaled again!" The third foal arrived a few days after the second one, and it was another female. The fourth and final one came a few days after the third one and was another male. The mares had all produced healthy foals, and the stallion had definitely proved his worth as well. The stallion tried to take all the credit, but the mares said, "Neigh." All the recent productivity at the ranch made for extremely busy months in May and June. Matt had to be sure that the mares had sufficient grain and hay so they were able to provide adequate nutrition for the foals. The foals would depend on the mares until they were weaned at four or five months of age. During this time, Matt kept a close eye on the broodmares to see when they would be able to mate again. Mares can give birth every year and often do so until they are in their early twenties. Horses generally live to be thirty-five or forty years old, with the oldest recorded horse living to age sixty-two.

That year, Matt put the first mare into the other corral with the stallion around May 1, with the other three getting their turns by May 20. Matt also had additional chores around the farm and was still doing surveying, too. He now rode alone to town to work at his office those two days a week to complete his recording of data and do other paperwork. Becky had taken a leave of absence from work starting in mid-May and was just hanging out at the farm most of the time.

During that busy time, Harvey had also been planting crops again, both on his own and his parents' properties. He was becoming a very industrious and capable man. He and his father also were continuing work on their two rural houses and were very near the completion of both. They decided to finish Harvey's first, as he wanted to move there so that he could more easily tend to the farming.

Then, about mid-June, Matt got a letter from his mother telling him that his father had passed away on May 30 due to complications from an infection. One of Matt's sisters and her family were going to move onto the Franklin horse farm in Kentucky to be with Matt's mom and help her with things. Matt wrote back with his condolences and with information about what had been happening in Bellevue. He assured them that he would send notice of the new baby as soon as it arrived. Once again, Matt was a bit distressed with a measure of guilt at having declined his father's request for him to return to Kentucky to live and to take over the horse farm management.

The rest of June went by, and along came July! Another July Fourth was rapidly approaching and would occur on Monday of the next week. They were all debating what they would do to celebrate, with everything up in the air due to Becky's pregnancy. Becky could tell that the time was getting near and shared that information with everyone else in both families. On Saturday, Clint went to the organizers of the big holiday cookout on Main Street and arranged to pick up enough food for six people on Monday. Then, he would be able to take it out to Matt and Becky's house in the country. The rest of Saturday and Sunday went by.

July Fourth started with Matt's going outside, as usual, to do his morning chores and check on the animals, particularly the young foals. Ruby had been staying overnight the past week or so just in case she was needed to help with the baby's delivery. When Matt came back in from his chores, Ruby had water boiling on the stove and told Matt that it was time. Matt immediately asked what he could do, and Ruby told him to go get a few more buckets of water and to keep boiling water as she needed it. She would let him know if she needed anything else. She also told him to keep an eye out for Sammy, to entertain him and feed him, and to make sure that he didn't come into the master bedroom.

Ruby disappeared into the bedroom, and Matt heard an occasional cry of pain and several subdued moans before Ruby came out for some fresh water. She already had a pile of towels in the bedroom with her. She took a couple of quick swigs of coffee and headed back in with Becky. There were more cries and then, all of a sudden, a new and very shrill cry, one of a newborn baby. Matt was beside himself with worry and didn't know what to do, but he stayed in the kitchen until Ruby came out and said, "You have a new son! He and Becky are both doing very well, and you can go in there now." Matt dashed for the bedroom and found a very exhausted-looking Becky holding the precious little package that was their new son. He sat on the edge of the bed, hugged Becky a bit awkwardly, then kissed her and kissed his son, thinking all the things that a father thinks when he first sees one of his newborn children.

He stayed in there with Becky for quite a while, and together, they were overjoyed and enchanted by the miracle that she was holding. She said to Matt, "We should name him after your father, Benjamin." Her statement, of course, made Matt teary eyed as he thought of the recent death of his father and of the new life now in front of him. Matt replied, "Your father has been extremely important to us both and we should also use his name. How about Clinton Benjamin Franklin? That sounds a little more natural that Benjamin Clinton Franklin."

So, within the first twenty minutes or so, they had settled on the name of the newest member of their family. Matt then went back out to the kitchen, got Sammy, and took him into the bedroom to meet his brother, and Sammy was elated with what he saw. He kissed the baby and kissed his new mommy, too. Ruby came in and put the baby into the nearby cradle, telling Becky that she should rest now as she had been through quite an ordeal. Becky knew better than to argue with her mother.

Back out in the kitchen, Matt told Ruby the new baby's name that he and Becky had agreed upon. Ruby thought that it was perfect and that Clint would be very pleased. Sammy asked when he could take the baby outside and get on the new swing set. They all sat and enjoyed one another, sharing more coffee for another hour, with Ruby going in once to check on things in the bedroom. She found both Becky and the baby asleep.

Right at ten thirty that morning, Clint and Harvey pulled in with their wagon and began bringing in the food from the town cookout. Clint looked at their faces and could tell that there was good news. Sammy said, "Mommy had her baby, and it's a boy!"

Matt added, "We named him Clinton Benjamin." Clint's eyes watered up, and he said that the namesake was a real honor for him.

Harvey said, "Whatever."

Ruby went back into the bedroom a little after eleven o'clock when the baby started crying. She came back out and said the baby was having breakfast. Sammy said, "What is he having?" They all laughed and told him it was something he was enjoying with his mommy. An hour or so later, Ruby went back in to check on Becky, who said she wanted to come out to join everyone. But Ruby convinced her that she should stay where she was for a while to rest and regain her strength.

Around three o'clock, Ruby went back in. Becky was awake again and the baby was starting to fuss a little, so she fed him again. Then, Ruby helped Becky get her robe on, and they went out to the kitchen. Clint gave his daughter a big hug, while Ruby went back into the bedroom and got the baby. Matt carried the cradle out to where they were. They all sat around the kitchen table and rejoiced in what had occurred that morning and then started having a holiday meal, which Ruby had kept warm on the stove. July Fourth would never be forgotten in this household, and the amazing thing about it was that everyone in the whole country would celebrate the young boy's birthday with him every year.

Harvey also had an interesting tidbit to share that he had learned at the school a year earlier. July Fourth was also the date that both Thomas Jefferson and John Adams had died, both occurring in the same year, 1826. They had both signed the Declaration of Independence and both later became president of the United States. Now, young Clinton Benjamin Franklin shared a significant date in history with those two men of distinction.

The rest of the summer rolled along. It rained quite a bit, and Harvey's crops were doing extremely well—so well, in fact, that he proposed to Bonnie in late August, and she accepted. They set a wedding date of November 5 to be sure that all the crops had been harvested by then and either stored or shipped somewhere to market. Harvey began furnishing his rural house about that same time, and Bonnie had some of her own things that she would bring with her into the marriage. On the main street, a couple of new businesses had been added, and the town constructed some additional storefronts for future additions.

Matt kept busy with his surveying, his recording, and also his attention to the horses. He also made time to spend with Becky and the two boys. After a few months, Sammy was still struggling with calling the baby Clinton. He said, "Krypton" or "Quentin," but he did better with calling his baby brother Benny. Eventually, this led to "Benjy," and as a result, everyone on both sides of the family started calling him Benjy.

Clint stayed busy at the smithy while also working on finishing up his own house and converting the former structure into a barn, as Matt and Harvey had already done. He and Ruby were hopeful about selling their house in town the following spring and finally moving out to the country to be near the rest of the family.

Harvey started harvesting in early September, and his dad and Matt, along with a couple of other neighbors, helped him when they could. He had a bumper crop and stored as much as he could in his own barn; gave some to Matt, even though Matt offered to pay him the market price; and gave some to his dad and mom. The rest he shipped to markets on the Missouri and turned a nice profit. Later, he opened a savings account at the bank so he would have funds available in future years that might not be as productive.

November 5 arrived, the wedding date for Bonnie and Harvey. They had selected Becky and Matt as their maid of honor and best man. When they asked, Becky said she would be delighted and honored to be Bonnie's maid of honor, and Matt felt it was now his turn to say, "Whatever." Harvey chose two other settlers to be his groomsmen, and Bonnie chose two other young ladies from church to be her bridesmaids. Sammy was again the ring bearer, but they also chose Bonnie's youngest sister as a flower girl, with flowers coming from one of the new stores on the main street. Preacher Devine conducted the service, which had many people in attendance, and they held a short reception right there in the church after the wedding ended. At that time of year, they were all a bit concerned about what the weather might be, but it turned out to be okay and everyone had a really good time, with most heading home before dark.

The rest of the year went by fast, with plenty of things to do and lots of meaningful activities. Thanksgiving was a huge event hosted by Harvey and Bonnie at their new house. Clint had gone out hunting and come home with a couple of nice turkeys, and they had one for Thanksgiving dinner, along with many vegetables that had been raised on the three farm properties, mainly tended by Ruby and Becky. Their garden had also produced quite a few pumpkins, and the three ladies made enough pumpkin pies to feed an army.

Christmas was an exceedingly pretty day, with snow falling lightly and an aura of peace in the air. They all went to church that morning and then over to Clint and Ruby's house for their Christmas gift exchange and Christmas dinner. The meal was highlighted by another delicious turkey with all the trimmings, followed by many pies. They all thanked God for their many blessings during 1859.

1860 — Happy Events and War Concerns

The year of 1860 emerged with gusto, with quite a bit of snow in January and some bitter cold to go with it. Fortunately, they all had stored an abundant supply of firewood before winter set in. February brought mixed weather, and March rolled around with several nice days followed by a couple of very windy and blustery ones.

Matt continued to take care of his growing herd of horses, and Clint kept working on his house and barn to get them completed. He often had help from Harvey and sometimes from Matt. In late March, Matt again began expecting new foals, and one arrived in early April. Clint finished his house, and they began making plans to sell their house in town and move out to the farm. About that same time, Harvey began his spring planting, doing his own property first and then his parents'. Matt was using all his property for horses. His other five broodmares all foaled before the end of third week of April, with four males and two females being born. In early May, he again began the process of watching the mares to see when they looked like they were ready to visit the stallion.

Near the end of April, Becky informed him that she was pregnant again and thought she would be due around the end of August. Once again, Matt had to write to his mother and say that they would not be able to visit that summer. He explained that Becky was due in late summer and that he would need to be home to watch the boys and to help Becky. He also mentioned that he would be quite busy with his growing horse herd. He sent along some pictures of the boys, plus family pictures from Harvey's wedding, Thanksgiving, and Christmas. Again, his mother wrote back that she understood and said that maybe he and Becky could arrange it the next summer, in 1861. She also told him all that was happening at their horse ranch and in the remainder of Kentucky, as opposing factions were becoming more heated against each other over the slavery issue.

The busy summer rolled on, with Clint and Ruby selling their house in town and moving to their farm. On September 4, Becky gave birth to a baby girl. They had given a lot of thought before the birth regarding a name. If it was a girl, they discussed using Amy as a first or middle name, but Matt shied away from the idea, thinking that perhaps it wasn't appropriate since he was now married to Becky. They discussed their mothers' names, Ruby and Susan, as well as using Bellevue in the name somehow. They asked Clint and Ruby for their thoughts. Ruby told them that she didn't want the baby named Ruby because she didn't really like her own name all that well. After additional discussions for a few days after the baby girl was born, they finally decided on her name: it was to be Sarah Rose Franklin. With her rosy little cheeks, it seemed like a very fitting name and one they hoped that Sammy would be able to pronounce.

The next week after the baby girl was born, Harvey began his fall harvest, and it proved to be almost as good as the year before. They were fully stocked up with grain, and that year he had added alfalfa to his crops. They had an ample supply of everything necessary to get them through the upcoming winter, especially Matt with his many horses.

They relaxed a bit at Halloween that year, as they'd had a good garden and pumpkin crop that year. Thanksgiving was festive, with lots of good food, and Christmas was another very special time, with all of them gathering together on Christmas Day as they had for the prior three years.

1861 – Civil War and Post-Civil War

January and February of 1861 were milder than they had been the previous two years. The month of March came about, and everyone began thinking about new planting and new horses. By late March, Harvey was already beginning to break ground for his crops and getting the fields leveled off. Matt was watching his mares, and they began foaling a few days earlier than the prior year, on March 29. Within three weeks, all six broodmares had dropped their foals and begun the task of feeding their offspring. About that same time, Harvey was getting close to being finished with the spring planting.

Abraham Lincoln had been elected president of the United States, and there was now increasing unrest and uncertainty about the future, even in the Nebraska Territory, which was on the periphery of the unrest. Matt had discussed it with Becky, and they had decided that he would go by himself to visit his mother and his sisters. Not only were there now three children under six years of age, but Matt continued hearing stories of possible problems in some of the states between Nebraska and Kentucky. He really did want to see his mother again, and he also wished to see his two sisters, whom he hadn't seen for seven or eight years. But a greater deciding factor was that Clint and Ruby now lived near them in the country, so Clint would manage the horses for Matt and Ruby would be available to help Becky with the kids. Matt decided he would leave soon after the foaling was complete and would return after spending two weeks with his family in Kentucky.

He left the ranch early in the morning on Monday, April 29. He rode his horse to the ferry, crossed the river on the ferry, and then took off across Iowa and into Illinois. From there, he angled southwest through Illinois to Kentucky. Traveling alone, he could make very good time, and he was in Kentucky nine days later, arriving at his mother's horse farm on the afternoon of May 8.

Matt spent the next two weeks visiting with his mother, his two sisters, and their families. He gave them many photographs of his family back in Bellevue, of his horses, and of the town itself. He also went over to the home of Jasper and Caroline Hughes one day to take them several pictures of Sammy, their grandson whom they had never seen. They were very grateful for his visit and for the pictures. They all promised one another that they would correspond in the future.

Matt's mother and sisters informed him of all the turmoil raging across the state over the slavery issue. Recently, word had arrived in their community that a civil war had now broken out, with the southern states attacking a fort controlled by the North at Fort Sumter, South Carolina. This had just occurred on April 12.

His family indicated that most local people were against slavery and were trending toward being on the side of the northern states, later called the Union. Other people supported slavery and tended toward supporting the southern states, which became known as the Confederacy. His mom was doing well, as were his sisters and their families. Their main concern was whether the looming war would affect them and, if so, how much. Meanwhile, with Matt visiting, they enjoyed reminiscing about when they were younger and catching up on things that had happened during the last eight years. They had a couple of meaningful discussions about his father, and both Matt's mother and his oldest sister told Matt how proud his father had been of him and what he had achieved. This revelation did a lot toward mending one of the heartaches that Matt had.

Matt was quite pleased to see everyone and to be able to catch up with his family, but he worried a bit about what might happen to them if the war escalated. They assured him that things would be okay, according to the information that they had received from leaders of the community. The leaders of Kentucky had already told other states that they wanted to remain neutral during this conflict and not be a part of it. His family assured Matt that things would be okay with all of them, and when his two weeks were over, he said his goodbyes and headed back for Nebraska on May 22.

He was stopped near Kentucky's border with Illinois when a couple of men on horses asked him who he was and what he thought about the slavery issue. They also wondered where he was going. Matt carefully answered the questions by saying, "I am not from around here. I live in the Nebraska Territory near the Missouri River. I was visiting family where I grew up, and now I am heading back home." That answer seemed to satisfy them, and they wished him a safe trip. But as he looked back, he noticed that they were following him and keeping a consistent distance away from him. After he had crossed the border into Illinois, he found that they were no longer following him. He was glad that they had not pressed the issue and asked him whom he had been visiting. He continued to be vigilant, checking his surroundings as he passed through Illinois and reached the border of Iowa. After that, he made good progress and arrived back at his home near Bellevue on June 1.

When he had left Kentucky, he did not know that this would be the last time that he would see his mother and that it would be many years before he would see his sisters again. He later learned that Kentucky's requested neutrality was honored at the beginning of the war, with South Carolina, Florida, Mississippi, Alabama, Georgia, Louisiana, and Texas being the first seven states to secede from the United States, followed later by Virginia, Arkansas, Tennessee, and

North Carolina. Toward the middle to later stages of the war, a third grouping was added, to include Missouri and Kentucky. Still, Kentucky's neutral status helped them to avoid becoming too heavily involved with any of the main fighting going on in other states. Most Kentucky citizens just wanted to stay out of the Civil War. No one at that time predicted that the Civil War would last for almost exactly four years, ending on April 9, 1865, when southern general Robert E. Lee surrendered to northern general Ulysses S. Grant at Appomattox Courthouse.

Back in Bellevue, the summer continued with all its required hard work, and the rest of the year passed by with the typical celebrations, holidays, and events that had occurred in previous years. Main Street was adding even more stores, and the town was continuing to grow and becoming an even more busy and important settlement.

Settlement and the town's population growth slowed during the Civil War as the number of wagon trains diminished. Fortunately, hardly any of the war reached as far west as the Nebraska Territory. The territory seemed to mostly comprise people who were against slavery, and a few of the younger settlers left to join the war efforts in other states farther east. About half of those who left to fight did not return to Bellevue.

During the war years, Bellevue's citizens and town leaders did a lot to make the town more livable for new settlers. They envisioned an improved quality of life after the terrible war ended. As the war came to a close, the main street was full of business locations. More than fifteen stores were now in operation, and several other storefront spaces were available for usage. The rural area outside Bellevue also had many more small farms now due to Matt's work with the surveying and as the town's land clerk. He was diligent in completing his work, and he had become quite well respected by everyone in the town, as well as by most people in the surrounding countryside.

Matt and Becky had another baby boy in 1864, which was to be their final child. Harvey and Bonnie also had two children during the war years, one in early 1862 and the next one in late 1864. Matt received word from his sister, Martha, in late 1863 that his mother had died. His sister also told him that their horse farm was still in operation and had remained safe for the most part, although a couple of military groups who had stopped there had "borrowed" some horses from them. Matt had also heard from Amy's parents a few times and had continued sending them pictures of Sammy and even a few of his entire family. They were grateful for his information and correspondence.

Finally, the war ended in April of 1865, and gradually the wagon trains began arriving on a little more regular basis again. Due to the proximity of the ferry that crossed the river from Iowa's bank over to Bellevue, this route was far more used by wagon trains than it had been for the fifteen previous years. As time went by, other families began leaving the wagon trains and settling in the Bellevue area. At last, in March of 1867, Nebraska was accepted as the thirty-seventh state in the union.

It was now the late spring of 1867. Matt was on one of his forays to find and survey some more land. As he rode over a rise, he saw down below him the mighty Missouri River flowing by. From the promontory on which he now sat looking at the river and the surrounding terrain, he began thinking about the ten years since their arrival in early June of 1857. He recalled his anguish at the time. He thought of the ideas that he had come up with and the work that he had put into making them move forward. He thought of his relationship with Becky as it had moved forward toward eventual marriage. He thought of his friendships with Clint, Ruby, and Harvey, and he also thought about all the new friendships he had gained since arriving in Bellevue. He thought of the progress that the town had made and about the bright future ahead for the community. He felt a sense of gratitude, but he also felt a real sense of accomplishment in what his part had been in the progress of the town and the surrounding area. He smiled and felt at peace with the world as he turned his horse and headed back to the town and family that he loved.

Epilogue

Fort Crook

I n 1891, Matt celebrated his sixtieth birthday, and Becky turned fifty-five. Samuel (who used to be called Sammy) was thirty-four, had married, and had two children. Like his father had been, Samuel was also now heavily involved in the community, doing the same kind of work his father used to do. Harvey was now fifty-two, and he and Bonnie had raised four children while maintaining a successful farming operation. Clint had passed away in 1887 at age eighty-two, and Ruby had passed away two years later, in 1889.

In 1891, the government built an army depot on the outskirts of Bellevue, first used as a dispatch point for Indian conflicts on the Great Plains and later as an airfield for the 61st Balloon Company of the Army Air Corps. This depot was named Fort Crook in honor of General George Crook, who had been a successful general through many Indian campaigns both in the Midwest and in the southwestern United States. Crook also had served at Fort Omaha, not too far north of Bellevue. A bronze statue of Crook is still there at Fort Omaha, as well as a building called the General Crook House. General Crook was buried in Arlington National Cemetery in 1898.

Fort Crook remained adjacent to Bellevue until 1946, but a major part of it became regularly used in 1918 as an aviation location for the Army Air Corps. On May 10, 1924, that aviation field was renamed Offutt Air Force Base in honor of First Lieutenant Jarvis Jennes Offutt, a native of nearby Omaha who had died on August 13, 1918, from injuries sustained when his SE-5 fighter plane crashed during a training flight near Valheureux, France.

On November 9, 1948, Offutt gained international prominence when it became the host base and national headquarters for the Strategic Air Command for the entire United States, moving from Andrews Air Force Base in Maryland. SAC headquarters still remains at Offutt Air Force Base in Bellevue today, playing a major part in helping guard our country from any potential threat, either foreign or domestic.

About the Author

Wm. Bruce McCoy worked in education for forty-five years. He started with fourteen years at Brownell-Talbot School in Omaha, then was athletic director and assistant principal at Bellevue West High School from 1979 to 1989 before going on to serve twenty years as the superintendent of three small school districts at Exeter, Nebraska; Winnebago, Nebraska; and Lewiston, Nebraska, where he retired in the summer of 2011 after fifteen years there. McCoy got his BA from Peru State College in 1965, his master's degree in guidance and counseling from the University of Nebraska at Omaha in 1970, and his doctorate in educational administration from the University of Nebraska at Lincoln in 1977.